BARE VIOLENCE

It figured that Canyon O'Grady would have both his guard and his pants down—after a long, long night with a bedmate like Sally Cole. But though the Senator's shapely secretary was fast asleep, Canyon sprang to life when he heard the intruder.

Canyon didn't have time to put on his clothes. He didn't have to.

All he needed was a Colt in his hand.

"I wouldn't move if I was you," he said.

Then the intruder made another mistake. Startled, he shouted, "What the hell—" and started firing his gun in the dark.

Muzzle flashes lit the room, and Canyon could see this was no time to be fancy. Every shot O'Grady fired was meant to kill . . .

CANYON O'GRADY RIDES ON

THE KILLERS' CLUB

by

Jon Sharpe

A SIGNET BOOK

SIGNET
Published by the Penguin Group
Penguin Books USA Inc., 375 Hudson Street,
New York, New York, 10014, U.S.A.
Penguin Books Ltd, 27 Wrights Lane, London W8 5TZ, England
Penguin Books Australia Ltd, Ringwood, Victoria, Australia
Penguin Books Canada Ltd, 10 Alcorn Avenue, Toronto, Ontario, Canada M4V 3B2
Penguin Books (N.Z.) Ltd, 182-190 Wairau Road,
Auckland 10, New Zealand

Penguin Books Ltd, Registered Offices:
Harmondsworth, Middlesex, England

First published by Signet, an imprint of New American Library,
a division of Penguin Books USA Inc.

First Printing, January, 1992

10 9 8 7 6 5 4 3 2 1

Canyon O'Grady

His was a heritage of blackguards and poets, fighters and lovers, men who could draw a pistol and bed a lass with the same ease.

Freedom was a cry seared into Canyon O'Grady, justice a banner of the heart.

With the great wave of those who fled to America, the new land of hope and heartbreak, solace and savagery, he came to ride the untamed wildness of the Old West.

With a smile or a six-gun, Canyon O'Grady became a name feared by some and welcomed by others but remembered by all . . .

*June, 1861, The District of Columbia,
where men's ambitions spread out as wide
as the Great Plains . . .*

1

The assassin closed his hand over the butt of the gun in his belt, but did not draw it. Not yet. He was simply reassuring himself of its presence. The feel of the wooden grips in his hand comforted him, for he was very nervous over what he was about to do. It wasn't that he had never killed a man before. On the contrary, he had killed many, but this was his first kill for the club and he wanted everything to go just right.

He stood in the center of the crowd of people waiting to see the great actor, Charles Henry Oliver, step from the Monarch Theater in Washington, D.C., fresh from another triumphant performance. At the moment, Oliver was the most famous actor on the American stage. He had performed to rave reviews in cities like New York, Philadelphia, and San Francisco, and he was in the process of taking Washington, D.C. by storm.

Charles Henry Oliver could hear the crowd waiting outside for him. He took one last look at himself in his dressing-room mirror, just to make sure that every hair was in place. He leaned close and critically examined his hair for signs of gray. At forty-one, he was very concerned that he might start showing his age. He didn't want that to happen, not when he was finally getting the recognition he deserved. He ran his finger over his mustache, then reached for his cape and swirled it around once—the way he did onstage—and draped it over his shoulders. He didn't want to keep his adoring public waiting too long.

"Charles," Walter Meade said, entering the room. Meade was Oliver's manager, and had been for many years. At fifty-five, the little gray-haired man had managed many actors and actresses, but none had achieved the success that Oliver had.

"I'm ready, Walter."

"I still say we should go out the stage entrance," Meade said worriedly. "There are a lot of people out front."

"Nonsense," Oliver said. "I can't disappoint them, Walter. Let's go."

"All right . . ." Meade said, shaking his head and leading the way.

This had been Charles Henry Oliver's third performance in Washington, D.C. He was not aware it was also his last.

There were a couple of policemen in front of the theater holding back the crowd, but they were concerned with people who simply wanted to touch the actor. There was no thought in either of their minds that anyone might want to kill him.

Officer Albert Nolan looked out over the crowd—mostly women—and shook his head.

"I don't understand it," he said to Officer Pat Wilson, who was standing next to him. "What makes this fella so great?"

"I don't know," Wilson said. "I ain't seen him myself. My wife and I don't go to the theater much."

Nolan, a young man of twenty-five, wasn't married and squired several of Washington's lovely young ladies around town, but like his older colleague, he had never been to the theater.

"Please, miss," Wilson said to a spinsterish woman, "move back."

"I want to see him," the woman said desperately.

"Please, ma'am," Wilson said. "He'll be out any minute now."

Wilson looked over at Nolan and rolled his eyes. Nolan just shrugged and then braced himself as a couple of young women pushed against him again. These women, however, were young and attractive. As they pressed against him he found himself thinking that there was worse duty he could have been assigned tonight.

The assassin caught his breath as he saw the front doors of the theater open. The crowd surged and he pushed his way to the front. He hadn't wanted to be in front while he waited, but now he needed to be as close as possible, to make sure that no one got in his way. He kept his right hand on the gun butt while he cleared a path for himself with his left.

The actor came out of the theater and paused before descending the steps. His carriage was waiting for him at the base of the steps, surrounded by admirers. The assassin suddenly realized that it would be very easy just to wait for the man to come to him. He changed his direction and started to push toward the carriage.

Charles Oliver loved the attention, but the crowd was getting larger and larger, and he realized belatedly that his manager might have been right about using the side entrance. This crowd could unintentionally trample him if he wasn't careful. He walked down the steps and stopped, just out of the crowd's reach, behind the two policemen, Meade next to him.

"Officers," Meade said, "you're gonna have to help Mr. Oliver get to his carriage."

Officer Wilson looked at Meade and said, "We're supposed to be controlling the crowd."

"If Mr. Oliver is injured, even slightly," Meade said, "I'll be speaking to your chief."

Wilson frowned, looking at Nolan, and said, "We better help him get to the carriage. The faster he gets to it, the faster he'll leave, and the crowd will disperse."

"All right," Nolan said. He looked at the actor. "You better walk between us, Mr. Oliver."

They started for the carriage . . .

* * *

The assassin had reached the carriage and was waiting. When he saw the policemen walking Oliver toward him he took a deep breath. Maybe he should have shot the man as he came out of the theater, but it was too late for that now. He would be as close to the policemen as he was to the actor when he pulled the trigger, but that couldn't he helped. Succeeding was much more important than succeeding and escaping.

As the three men pushed through the crowd toward him, the assassin drew the gun from his belt . . .

Nolan was in the lead, with Oliver right behind him. Wilson came next and Meade was close behind him, keeping up a steady stream of chatter that was supposed to be helpful.

"Watch that woman . . . look out for that lady, she's trying to grab him . . . come on, Officers, push . . ."

As they neared the carriage, Meade put his hands on Wilson's back and started pushing. Already annoyed that the man kept jabbering in his ear, Wilson looked back and said, "Don't do that!"

Hearing his partner, Nolan turned his head. "What's the matter?"

"I'm sorry!" Meade said, removing his hands from Wilson's back as if they had been scalded.

Wilson turned his head to reply to his partner, and that was when he saw the man with the gun. If he and Nolan hadn't both turned their heads at that moment, they might have seen the man before he drew his gun. As it was, the man was already extending the gun, pointing it at the actor. In that position, the gun was right next to Nolan's face.

"Hey!" Wilson shouted. "Watch out!"

"Wha—" Nolan said. He turned his head just as the man with the gun fired. The muzzle flash blinded Nolan, but he reached out convulsively with both arms and wrapped them around the gunman.

"I got 'im!" he shouted as he and the gunman fell to the ground together.

Charles Henry Oliver didn't know what was happening. All he was aware of was the burning pain in his chest, and then he was falling.

The assassin struggled with the young policeman as the spectators screamed and surged away. Escape was impossible now; he was trying to free his gun arm so he could put the muzzle of the gun in his mouth.

"I got 'im!" the younger policeman yelled again, but the assassin finally freed his gun arm and struck Nolan a blow to the head. He scrambled from beneath the man and hurriedly lifted the gun to his mouth. Suddenly someone jarred his arm. The barrel of the gun struck him in the mouth, mashing his lips and breaking two teeth, but before he could pull the trigger someone grabbed his wrist, flipped him over onto his stomach, and twisted the arm up behind his back.

"No you don't," Officer Pat Wilson said. "You ain't gettin' off that easy!"

2

Canyon O'Grady sat waiting patiently outside the Oval Office for President Abraham Lincoln to call him in. The big redheaded agent didn't mind waiting. He knew how busy Lincoln was. It had only been a matter of months since the President had taken over the office from the previous Commander-in-Chief, James Buchanan, and there was still much to be done before Mr. Lincoln was "comfortable" in his new job.

Canyon had very much enjoyed serving under President Buchanan. He had respected the man and, even more than that, had genuinely liked him. He did not know Mr. Lincoln well enough to say that he liked him, but he had already built up a healthy respect for the new President. Lincoln had a way of speaking his mind that appealed to Canyon, since he himself had that very same attribute.

The door to the Oval Office opened abruptly, and Major General Rufus Wheeler appeared in the doorway. Canyon stared at the man with no hint of surprise at seeing him there.

"Come in, Canyon," Wheeler said with a wave of his hand.

Canyon rose and entered the Oval Office.

Lincoln was standing behind his desk, staring out the window at a portion of the White House garden. His hands were clasped behind his back, and he stood ramrod straight.

Canyon positioned himself in front of the President's desk and waited. General Wheeler, off to one side, cleared his throat.

Lincoln turned and looked at them as if surprised to find them there. Canyon realized that the President must have been deep in thought.

"Mr. O'Grady," he said, "thank you for responding so promptly to my summons."

"It's my duty to do that, sir."

"Yes, well," Lincoln said, turning completely around now. His hands remained clasped behind his back. "Thank you, nevertheless."

"Yes, sir."

"Sit down, sit down," Lincoln said. "Would you like a drink?"

"No, thank you, sir," Canyon said, choosing a straight-backed chair instead of one of the sofas in the room. "I'd really just rather find out what this is all about. I've only just returned from—"

"Yes, yes," Lincoln said, gently but firmly cutting Canyon off. "I realize you've only been back in Washington a short time after your last assignment, but this . . . this is very important, or I wouldn't have called you here."

"I'm sure it is, sir," Canyon said, and then added, "whatever it is."

Wheeler threw Canyon a look designed to quiet him, and the agent waited.

"Have you heard about the murder of Charles Henry Oliver?" Lincoln asked.

"The actor?" Canyon said. "I read about it in the papers." He was frowning. Surely the killing of an actor wasn't what he had been called here about.

As if reading his mind, Lincoln said, "Yes, that's why I've called you here."

"Mr. President," Canyon said, "I'm sure the murder of any man is a tragedy, but what could it be about this particular man's murder that would interest the United States Government?"

"I'll tell you, Mr. O'Grady," Lincoln said. He took his hands from behind his back, picked up a folder from his desk, and brandished it. "It was only the most recent of several such assassinations."

"Assassinations?"

"That's what we're calling them," General Wheeler said.

"In the past three months," Lincoln went on, "there have been six assassinations of prominent American citizens around the country."

Lincoln looked at Wheeler. Clearly, he wanted the officer to continue.

Wheeler began to speak, ticking off the victims on his fingers.

"In San Francisco, a prominent businessman was shot to death outside his home in front of his family; in Mississippi, a well-respected lawman was shot down on the street in full view of the townspeople; in Wisconsin, a leading preacher was stabbed to death in front of his shocked congregation; in Minnesota, an important banker was shot and killed in his own bank in front of staff and customers; in Kentucky, a powerful rancher was shot and killed by a man who had only days before been hired as a hand; and now, here in Washington, a famous actor is gunned down in front of a crowd of fans."

"I don't like what's happening, O'Grady," Lincoln said. "People are being killed for no apparent reason."

"No reason?" Canyon asked. He looked at Wheeler. "Haven't the killers been questioned?"

"Each of the first five killers," Wheeler said, "did not survive. In San Francisco, the victim's partner shot and killed the assassin. In Mississippi and Wisconsin, the assassin was killed by angry mobs; in Minnesota, bank guards shot and killed the assassin, and in Kentucky, the man was killed by the other ranch hands."

"None of them were taken alive?" Canyon said, surprised.

"In each case," Wheeler said, "witnesses have stated that the assassin was not even attempting to flee."

"Wait a minute," O'Grady said. "You're telling me that the killers didn't try to get away?"

"More than that," Wheeler said. "They didn't even try to defend themselves."

"That's crazy."

"The whole thing is crazy," Lincoln said, "and I want it stopped. I have all I can do to try and avoid a war within our nation, Mr. O'Grady. I can't be worrying about madmen being on the loose, killing prominent citizens. My God, how long before a politician is a victim?"

Canyon knew some politicians he thought should be victims, but he said nothing. He knew what President Lincoln meant.

"I want you to look into this for me, Mr. O'Grady," the President said. "Would you do that for me?"

"Mr. President," Canyon said, "I'm really not a detective."

"I'm aware of that," Lincoln said, "but I happen to think you are the best man for the job. Now, I'm not going to order you to do this, but I'd appreciate it very much if you would handle it for me."

Canyon looked at Wheeler for a moment, but the man did not respond in any way.

"Well, of course, Mr. President," Canyon said. "I wouldn't ever refuse you."

"Thank you, Mr. O'Grady," Lincoln said, "I appreciate that. General, why don't you and Mr. O'Grady continue this briefing in your office?"

"Of course, sir," Wheeler said. "O'Grady?"

"And, of course, you'll keep me informed," Lincoln said to O'Grady's superior.

"Of course, sir," Wheeler replied. "Fully informed."

"Gentlemen," President Abraham Lincoln said, "I rest assured that this matter is in capable hands. Good day."

Canyon followed Wheeler to his office, questions running through his mind. He had committed himself to solving these seemingly unconnected murders, but he had no idea how to go about it. Victims, killers—they were all dead. There wasn't anyone to talk to!

He entered Wheeler's office and shut the door behind them.

"Sit down," Wheeler said.

"I'm not a detective, General."

"You told the President that."

"Now I'm telling you," Canyon said. "I don't have much to go on here. I mean, who is there even to talk to?"

"Stop complaining for a moment and think, Canyon," Wheeler said.

"It's a little early in the day for that," Canyon said, but then he fell silent.

"Wait," he said after a moment, "there are five victims and five dead killers."

"Right."

"This actor fella . . ."

"Charles Henry Oliver."

"He's victim number six."

"Right."

Canyon leaned forward and asked, "What happened to killer number six?"

"Aha," Wheeler said with no trace of humor. "He tried to put his gun in his mouth and pull the trigger."

"What happened?"

"Two policemen stopped him."

"And?"

"He ended up with some broken teeth and swollen lips, but he's alive."

"What were the policemen doing there?"

"Crowd control."

"Two policemen?"

"It was a small crowd."

"Why didn't they stop him before he shot the actor?" Canyon asked.

"Maybe you should ask them that," Wheeler said. "They're expecting you."

"What about the assassin?" Canyon said. "Can I talk to him?"

"Sure," Wheeler said. "The police are ready to cooperate with you."

"It's all arranged, huh?"

"All arranged."

Canyon shook his head and said, "I hate being predictable."

3

Canyon left the White House and went directly to police headquarters. When he presented himself at the front desk he was shown to the office of Lieutenant Rollo Dugan.

Dugan was a big, barrel-chested man in his forties who sat behind his desk with a decidedly unpleasant look on his face.

"So . . . you're the government man."

"I guess so."

"O'Grady, right? Canyon O'Grady?"

"That's my name, Lieutenant," Canyon said. "I'd like to speak to the two officers who—"

"You're the man I'm supposed to cooperate with, right?" Dugan said.

"I would hope so."

"You're real damn polite, aren't you?"

Canyon took a moment to compose himself. He knew that Dugan was baiting him. The man obviously was upset about being ordered to cooperate with a "government man." He was trying to goad Canyon into an explosion of anger, anything so that he could refuse to talk to him.

Finally Canyon said, "Not always."

"When are you not polite?"

"When I'm talking to a pigheaded cop who would rather start an argument than solve six murders."

"Who do you think—what did you say?"

"About what?"

"Six murders, did you say?"

"That's right," Canyon said, "in six different parts of the country. Yours—the actor last night—was the sixth. Now, if we can solve this—all of these—you could end up the next chief of police."

Dugan stared at him, and for a moment Canyon thought that he'd overdone it.

"I'll have the two officers come in here. You can use my office," the lieutenant finally said, standing up. He walked around the desk to the door, then turned and said to Canyon, "Uh, can I stay while you talk to them?"

"Sure," Canyon said. "We're in this together, aren't we?"

"There was just too damn much happening at one time," Officer Pat Wilson said.

"We just saw him too damn late," Officer Albert Nolan said.

From the look of Nolan's face, he hadn't seen much of anything. He had powder burns around his eyes, and although it wasn't all that bright in the room, he was squinting.

"Who stopped him?" Canyon asked.

"I did," Nolan said. "I couldn't see, but I just reached out and grabbed him."

"Then what happened?"

"We fell to the ground, and he hit me with his gun," Nolan said, touching the bandage on the side of his head.

"Then what happened?"

Wilson took up the story from there.

"Bastard tried to put his gun in his mouth," the older policeman said. "He was gonna blow his own head off. I stopped him, and arrested him." Wilson looked at Nolan and added, "We arrested him."

"I wish we'd been able to save the actor," Albert Nolan said.

"It wasn't your fault," Canyon told him. "You fellas did good work."

"Sure," Nolan said glumly.

"Did the man say anything?" Canyon asked.

"When?"

"Whenever. Before he fired the shot, or after you arrested him?"

"I didn't hear him say anything," Wilson answered.

"Neither did I," Nolan said.

"Come to think of it," Wilson commented, "he didn't say anything at all, not even after we brought him in."

Canyon looked at Lieutenant Rollo Dugan, who said, "As far as I know, he still ain't said anything."

Canyon nodded and looked at the two policemen. Wilson was wearing his uniform, but Nolan was dressed in street clothes.

"You fellas can go," Canyon said. "Thanks for talking with me."

They both rose, and Wilson said, "If there's anything we can do to help you, you let us know, huh?"

"I'll do that, Officer. Thanks."

The two policemen left the room and Canyon turned to look at the lieutenant.

"I'm ready to talk to the killer now."

Lieutenant Dugan took Canyon to the room where they had put the assassin for Canyon's interrogation. As Canyon entered he saw a man sitting in a straight-backed chair in the center of an otherwise empty room. The man sat with shoulders slumped and head hanging. There was one uniformed policeman in the room with him.

"You can go," Dugan said to the policeman. "Wait outside."

"Yes, sir."

As the policeman left, O'Grady approached the seated man.

"Do we know his name?" he asked Lieutenant Dugan.

"No," Dugan said. "He had no identification on him, and he won't tell us his name."

O'Grady put his hand beneath the man's chin and tilted his face up so he could see him. The man's face was bruised and battered, but Canyon decided not to make an issue of that. It could have happened during the arrest. In fact, the skinned right cheek could have been the result of the man being wrestled to the ground.

What was of more interest to the agent was the fact that the man did not look at him. Either that, or he genuinely didn't see him. His eyes appeared glazed, looking at nothing in particular except perhaps something that only he could see.

"Is he drugged?" Canyon asked.

Dugan shook his head.

"We had him examined by a doctor," the lieutenant said. "He isn't drugged and he isn't drunk. He's just been like that since we brought him in."

Canyon stared into the man's face and asked, "Can you hear me?"

There was no reply.

"Hey! Hello! Can you understand what I'm saying?"

Nothing.

"You see what we've been up against?" Dugan said. "He hasn't said a word, and we don't know who he is. What we do know, though, is that he definitely killed the actor. I mean, there were a lot of witnesses. He's gonna hang for it for sure."

While the lieutenant was speaking O'Grady had kept his eyes on the killer's face.

"That doesn't seem to bother him, does it?" he asked the policeman.

"I guess not."

Canyon turned to leave, but as an afterthought he reached out, took hold of the man's bruised and scraped cheek, and pinched it . . . hard. The man did not react to the pain at all.

"I've seen enough," Canyon said. "You can put him back in his cell."

Before leaving the police station Canyon thanked Lieutenant Dugan for all his cooperation. The lieutenant failed to notice the agent's sarcastic tone.

"You'll let me know what you find out, right?" Dugan said.

"Of course, Lieutenant," Canyon said. "We're partners, aren't we?"

When Canyon returned to his rooms that evening he found a message from General Wheeler saying that he wanted to see the agent right away. Canyon had intended to have a quiet dinner and then study the files he had been given on the other murders. He decided to forgo dinner but to let Wheeler wait while he at least made a cursory examination of the files.

At a glance all he could see that the victims had in common was that they were all prominent in one way or another, and they were all men. A couple were well known in their particular town or county, some in their state. The actor was beginning to achieve national acclaim. They were of different ages and sizes; some were rich and some—like the preacher—were not. The files would yield him nothing else until he had the time to study them.

He put on his hat and left from the White House.

In Wheeler's office the superior officer asked Canyon what he had found out from the killer.

"Nothing," Canyon replied. "The man either can't or won't talk. He looks like he's been drugged, or maybe hypnotized—"

"Hypnotized?" Wheeler said. "That's ridiculous!"

"I don't think it's something we should disregard," Canyon said.

"Well, if you want to waste your time looking into that, it's up to you. I called you here for a different reason."

"And what's that?"

"Senator Harrison Brown is making a personal appearance here in Washington tomorrow. He'll be speaking publicly on the subject of slavery."

"For or against?"

"I believe he's for it. He's from the South."

Canyon wasn't really familiar with the Senator or his opinions, but none of that seemed to matter at the moment.

"What's that mean to me?"

"The President is afraid that there might be an attempt on the Senator's life. He wants you to stay with the Senator until he's finished speaking."

"I thought he wanted me to look into these other murders."

"The President sees this as part of the same matter," Wheeler said.

"How does he figure that?"

"I suppose because the Senator is rather prominent," Wheeler said.

"Using that logic, the entire Senate, the House, and the President himself are potential victims."

"That's exactly how the President feels," Wheeler said. "However, Brown will be making a well-attended public appearance tomorrow, and it has attracted considerable publicity. He'll be in a perfect position to be assassinated."

Canyon really couldn't argue with that.

"I suggest you go to the Senator's hotel tonight and stay with him right through his speech tomorrow afternoon. Keep him alive."

Canyon sighed. "All right. What hotel?"

"The Plaza."

"Where else?" the agent said, standing up.

"After the Senator's speech you can go ahead and pursue your, uh, various angles on this case," Wheeler said. "The Senator has been informed that you'll be coming tonight. Let me warn you that he's, uh, not very happy with the arrangement."

"I have the files on the other murders in my room," Canyon said. "Would you send someone there to get them and bring them to me at the Senator's hotel? I'd like to go over them thoroughly as soon as possible."

"No problem," Wheeler said, and accepted Canyon's key. "Do you need anything else?"

The agent touched his Colt and said, "No, I have everything else I'll need for this assignment."

Canyon made two more stops before he went to the Senator's hotel.

The first was at police headquarters, where he made arrangements for someone to see the assassin.

"Is this another government man?" Lieutenant Dugan asked.

"It's just someone I'm recruiting to help us," Canyon said. "He won't need to see the killer for very long."

"All right. I'll just—"

"And he'll need to see him alone."

Dugan didn't like that, but he finally agreed.

Canyon's second stop was at a small theater on K Street to talk to a man whose performances there were drawing considerably less attention than those of the now-deceased Charles Henry Oliver. A lady friend had told Canyon about the man, whose name was Harry Barlow. He was supposedly a hypnotist.

Canyon was waiting in Barlow's dressing room when the man returned from his performance. He identified himself and told the man what he needed. Barlow, a tall, painfully thin man in his forties, was impressed with the fact that he was being asked to help the United States Government. He smoothed his already slicked-back black hair with one hand and said that he would be happy to assist in any way. Canyon told Barlow that he would make all the arrangements, and that they would speak again the following day.

That angle now covered, Canyon left the small theater and headed for the Washington Plaza Hotel.

4

The door to Senator Brown's hotel suite was opened by a lovely young woman who introduced herself as Sally Cole. She said that she was the Senator's executive assistant.

"What exactly does a senator's executive assistant do, Miss Cole?" Canyon asked.

"Well, at the moment, Mr. O'Grady," she replied, "I'm to show you to the Senator's office."

Sally Cole appeared to be in her early thirties. She was tall and blonde, although at the moment her blonde hair was clasped behind her head in a modest and very businesslike bun. She was wearing a severe dress that could not quite hide the full thrust of her breasts or the flare of her hips. She was staring at Canyon O'Grady with a speculative look on her face which, he suspected, matched perfectly the look on his own face.

"Well then, Miss Cole, why don't you lead the way?" he finally suggested.

She indicated a hall and said, "Right this way, please."

He followed her down the hall, admiring the way her hips and buttocks moved. She stopped at a door, knocked on it, then opened it without waiting for a reply.

"Senator Harrison Brown," she said, "this is Canyon O'Grady."

"All right, Sally," Senator Brown said from behind a small writing desk, "that will be all."

"Yes, sir."

Sally Cole withdrew and Canyon approached the desk. It

was rather obvious, as the Senator did not bother to rise or extend a hand, that the man was not happy with Canyon's presence. The Senator was about fifty-five or so, with a shock of salt-and-pepper hair that was more salt than pepper and would probably be totally white within a couple of years. His ruddy face was crisscrossed with deep-set lines, and he sported a pair of piercing, startlingly sky-blue eyes.

"I'm not happy about this arrangement, O'Grady," the Senator said.

"So I understand, sir," Canyon said. "To be truthful, neither am I. There are other things I'd rather be doing tonight and tomorrow."

"Indeed?" the Senator said. Now he studied the agent in a speculative manner which did not at all match that of his executive assistant. "Well, I appreciate your candor."

"If we could just go over your schedule for tomorrow, sir," Canyon said, "I'll get out of your way."

"You're not going to stay by my side every second?" Senator Brown asked.

"I don't think that will be necessary, sir," Canyon said. "Do you?"

"I'm liking you more and more every minute, O'Grady," Senator Brown said.

"That pleases me, sir."

The Senator frowned, trying to tell whether or not Canyon was being sarcastic.

The two men went over the Senator's itinerary for the following day, which would end with his speech in front of the White House in the afternoon.

"What is your opinion on the slavery question, Mr. O'Grady?" the Senator asked.

"My opinion has more to do with preserving the Union, Senator," Canyon said. "I'm against war, and against any groups that would call for our country to go to war against itself."

Senator Brown's look said that he was no longer liking Canyon O'Grady more and more.

"Is there a room for me in the suite, Senator?" Canyon asked.

"As a matter of fact, there is," Brown said. "I'll have Miss Cole show it to you." He made no move to get up and summon Miss Cole. Instead he added, "Uh, why don't you go and find her and tell her to do that?"

"Fine," Canyon said. "I assume, Senator, that I don't have to tell you not to leave the suite, or the hotel, without me?"

"I don't want to do this, O'Grady," the Senator said, "but since I've agreed, I intend to do it right. No, you don't have to tell me that."

"Good," Canyon said. "Well, sir, I expect I'll see you at dinner."

"You won't," Brown said. "I'll be dining right here at my desk. You and Miss Cole will have to fend for yourselves."

That suited him. He left the man's office and went to find Miss Cole so that they could start fending.

He became well acquainted with the suite before he finally located Sally Cole again. She was seated at a desk in a room that had book-lined walls.

"Hello," he said.

She looked up from her work and for just a moment she had a line down the center of her forehead, from frowning in concentration. When she saw him she smiled, and the line disappeared.

"Hi. Finished already?"

"For now," Canyon said. "Your boss doesn't like me very much, I'm afraid."

"He just doesn't like the idea of having a bodyguard," she said, then added, "or did he ask you to comment on the slavery issue?"

"He did."

"Well, you look like a man who wouldn't be in favor of such a thing, so I think I know why he doesn't like you."

"What about you?"

"What about me?"

"How do you feel about the slavery issue?"

She smiled and folded her hands in front of her on the desk.

"I have a deal with the Senator," she said. "I'll work for him, and he'll never ask me to comment on that question. I'd like to make the same deal with you."

"That's fine with me," Canyon said, "but you don't work for me, so you're going to have to offer me something else in return."

She stared at him for a moment with an amused look on her face and then said, "Mr. O'Grady—"

"Canyon, please."

"Oh, yes," she said, "I can see that you probably do very well for yourself with the ladies."

"Really?" he asked. "How well am I doing now?"

"Quite well," she said. "Was there something you wanted when you came in?"

He hesitated before answering, and was rewarded by a flush of color that crept into her face.

"The Senator said that you would show me to my room," he finally said.

"Oh," she said, rising, "of course. You'll be staying with us."

"Just for this one night."

"I see."

As she came around the desk he said, "He also said that he would be having dinner in his office and that we would have to fend for ourselves."

"Well," she said, sounding eager, "we could go out—"

"I'm sorry," he said, "but I can't leave the suite. You understand."

"Oh, of course," she said, "how foolish of me. Well, I'll just go downstairs and order dinner and have it brought up for us."

"After you show me to my room."

"Oh," she said, shaking her head at herself, "you must

forgive me. I'm not usually this flustered. I'm really a very orderly person."

"I can see that, Miss Cole," he said, "and I'm honored to be the reason that you're so flustered."

"Oh, but you're not—I mean you are, but—oh, my, you've done it again, haven't you?"

"I'm sorry, Miss Cole."

"Please," she said, "call me Sally."

"If you'll show me to my room, Sally, I'll get settled in."

"Come with me, then," she said, leading the way out of the room. "And while you settle in, I'll order dinner. Is there anything in particular you would like?"

"Oh, I think I'll leave that to you," he said. "I have the feeling we have a lot of the same tastes."

He was walking behind her and couldn't see her face, but since her hair was pinned up he could see the back of her neck, and noted that the remark had made her blush once again.

Dinner was pleasant, and Canyon found out a lot about Sally Cole while they were eating. She had been born in Philadelphia, educated in Washington. When she finished school she decided to live in Washington and had worked for many public servants as secretary and assistant before she'd started working with Senator Harrison Brown about five years earlier. During the course of the conversation Canyon was able to figure out that she was twenty-seven or -eight. He had originally guessed her as being older, but he attributed that to her self-assurance and her appearance. While beautiful, she also exhibited undeniable class, and classy, confident women often appeared older than they were.

On the other hand, while she asked a lot of questions, Sally Cole was not able to find out a whole lot about Canyon O'Grady, and that frustrated her.

"Do you practice being so evasive when you're asking questions?" she asked him toward the end of dinner.

"It's just something that comes naturally."

Sally had ordered pheasant for dinner, with various vegetables and a salad, and with the meal the hotel had supplied a waiter. At that moment the waiter approached the table and filled their wineglasses full once again.

"The suite has a balcony," she said. "Why don't we take the last of our wine out there?"

"Sounds like a fine idea."

Sally told the waiter that they were finished, but asked him to send someone up in the morning to clean away the debris. She made sure that he left the suite before she and Canyon walked out onto the balcony.

Looking out over Washington, Sally said, "It's an exciting city, isn't it?"

"Yes, it is."

"You can feel the undercurrent of power."

"Political power, you mean."

"Well, of course," she said, turning to face him. "In this town, what other kind is there?"

"I suppose you're right."

Canyon didn't like politics. There was much too much subterfuge and even blatant lying involved for his taste. He knew better, however, than to discuss his views, especially with a beautiful woman, and he was grateful when *she* changed the subject.

"So," she said, "tell me about your women."

"What women?"

"Oh, come now," she said. "You must have many conquests."

"Oh, conquests," he said. "Yes, I've had my share of conquests, but when you asked me to tell you about my women it sounded as if I had lots of wives or girlfriends to talk about."

"No wives?"

He shook his head. "Not even one."

"No regular girlfriends?"

"None."

"Why is that?"

"I move around too much."

"Ah, then you must have seen many exciting cities all over the country."

"I've been to a few."

"New York?"

"Yes."

"San Francisco?"

"Many times."

"New Orleans?"

"Once or twice."

"And you've had women in every city?"

He smiled. "One or two."

"You're a rogue, Canyon O'Grady," she said. "I can see that . . . and you're probably not to be trusted."

"Oh, I can be trusted," he said, "I just can't be relied on to be in any one place for any significant amount of time."

She moved closer to him and put her glass down on the balcony ledge.

Taking hold of his lapels, she asked, "Well, can I count on you to be here for—oh, the next few hours?"

He put his own glass down and laid his hands lightly on her hips.

"For the whole night, at least," he said.

She smiled and lifted her chin and he leaned down to kiss her. She touched her lips softly to his and pressed her body against him. Her breasts were firm against his chest, and her tongue blossomed sweetly in his mouth.

She moved her mouth just far enough away from his to be able to speak.

"I don't think this is the place to be doing this," she whispered.

He laughed and asked, "Do you know a better place?"

"Come with me," she said, taking his hand.

She led him from the balcony to the door to her room, which was situated near his. Both their rooms were well away from the Senator's.

"What about the Senator?" Canyon asked.

Sally kissed him and whispered, "Let him get his own girl."

5

Inside her room Sally wasted no time. Even as she was turning to face him she was removing her clothes and urging him to do the same.

"Hurry," she said breathlessly, "hurry . . ."

He hurried, but she was undressed before he was and he paused to admire her body. The lamp in the room was turned up just enough for him to see her. Her breasts were large and firm, the wide pink nipples already swollen with desire. Her hips were wide, her thighs deliciously full. Her pubic mound was even paler blonde than the hair on her head. In the light from the lamp it seemed to glow.

"Hurry, damn you!" she said, and her hands were at him, pulling his clothes from him. When she yanked down his shorts his member sprang free, and now it was her turn to stop and admire.

"Oh, my," she said, sinking to her knees, "it's beautiful . . . so beautiful." She touched his penis as if it were a treasure, sliding her fingers up the underside where it was sensitive, causing it to jump, and then over the head.

"Ooh," she crooned, "I knew you'd be beautiful all over from the moment I saw you."

She placed her hands on the back of his thighs and then ran them up until she was rubbing her palms over the cheeks of his buttocks. She moved around behind him and began to pepper his butt with hot kisses, mixing in a lick here and there, crooning to him all the while about how lovely his body was. She bit his right cheek just as she slid her hands around to the front, one cupping his balls, the other grasping his penis and pumping it, slowly at first, and then more quickly. Canyon braced his legs and reached behind him for her.

"Sally . . ." he said warningly.

"Oh, I know, darling," she said, kissing his right hip and then sliding around so that she could kiss and lick his flat belly. "I know, we don't want to waste it . . . and we won't."

She was in front of him now and he put his hands on her shoulders as she took him into her mouth. Slowly, she began to move her mouth on him, her head bobbing, and then the tempo began to speed up. Canyon felt the rush in his legs, felt himself swelling even more in her mouth. She had her hands on his buttocks now, squeezing them, kneading them, and then grasping them firmly and pulling him to her as she sensed he was about to explode. When he finally did he groaned aloud—hoping very briefly that the Senator would not be walking by the room at that very moment. She moaned appreciatively as he filled her mouth, and only when she had drained him did she allow him to pull free.

"Oh, God," she said, "you're such a delicious man. I knew you would be." She ran her hands up over his chest and said, "I hope there's more where that came from."

"Plenty more," he said, grasping her hands and pulling her to her feet, "I just need about ten minutes to rest."

"What do you mean, 'rest'?" she said, laughing. "I did all the work. Come on." She reversed their grips so that she was holding his wrists, and pulled him toward her bed.

"Sally—"

"Come on," she said again, "you can rest, but you can do it while you're fiddling with me. Come on, damn it, I want you to touch me!"

He allowed himself to be pulled to the bed and then she released him and crawled in beside him. She settled down on her back and said, "Come on, Canyon. I want your hands on me . . . I want your mouth, your tongue . . ."

She was a demanding woman, and he fully intended to supply what she was demanding.

In another part of the city, in another hotel room, a man named Carl Peyton nervously awaited the arrival of another man. He paced the floor, rubbing his hands together, until there was a knock at this door. Then he stopped and stared at it. Only when there was a second knock did he walk to the door and open it.

"I'm not pleased, Peyton," the other man said as he entered the room.

"I know, Mr. Lawrence—"

"Shut the damned door!"

"Yes, sir," Peyton said, swinging the door shut with a hard push.

"What happened?" Talbot Lawrence demanded.

Peyton was the physically larger of the two men, but it was he who was intimidated by the presence of the other.

"They caught Dawson and took him alive, sir."

"I *know* that, damn it! What I don't know is how? Why? Why didn't Dawson kill himself before allowing himself to be taken?"

"Well, as I understand it, he tried to, sir. They were just able to stop him."

"None of our people have ever been taken alive before, Peyton. I don't want this to be a setback."

"Oh, it's not, sir, I can assure you," Peyton said. "I mean, he did the job, he killed Oliver."

"If he talks—"

"He won't, I swear to you. In fact, given half a chance in jail he'll finish the job there."

"He'd better," Lawrence said, pointing a finger at Peyton, "because if he doesn't the money that's been funding this project will stop coming. Is that understood?"

"Perfectly, sir."

"I'm leaving now," Lawrence said. "Is everything set for tomorrow?"

"Yes, sir."

"It better go off as planned."

"It will."

"I'll be watching Thursday's newspapers, Peyton," Lawrence warned. "I had better read something good in them."

"You will, sir," Peyton said as Lawrence opened the door. "I promise."

Lawrence turned. "I respect men who keep their promises, Peyton," he said.

"Yes, sir."

"Do you know what I do to men who don't?"

"Uh, no, sir."

"Believe me," Lawrence said, "you don't want to."

Police Officer Joe Evans looked at Officer Dave Wells and said, "Did you see that fella who was in here before?"

"The hypnotist guy?"

"Yeah," Evans said. "Whataya suppose he was doing here?"

"I don't know. Maybe they expected this guy to talk to him."

"Well he didn't," Evans said. "The hypnotizer—or whatever he is—went in and talked to him for a while, and the guy didn't respond to him any more than he did to anyone else. I mean, this is the weirdest killer I ever seen. He just don't talk."

"How many killers you seen, Joe?"

"Well . . . not that many, but this is the weirdest one!"

"Well, that ain't our problem," Wells said. "Let's get him back to his cell and get something to eat."

They opened the door to the room where the assassin was being held and both walked in. The scene that greeted them froze them for a full three seconds. The killer was still sitting in his chair with his hands tied behind him, but his face was turning blue, he was frothing at the mouth, and before either of them could move he keeled over and fell to the floor.

"Jesus," Evans said, "what the hell—"

Wells reacted first, moving to the body and kneeling next to it.

"What happened to him?" Evans asked.

"Jesus," Wells said, "this guy's dead."

"What?"

Still on his knees next to the body, Wells looked back at Evans over his shoulder and said, "I think he swallowed his tongue."

Canyon leaned over Sally and his lips flitted over her swollen nipples. At the same time his hand moved down over her belly and ran through her pale pubic thatch until his fingertips encountered her hot, moist portal. He dipped his fingers into her, sucking at the same time on her right nipple. She caught her breath and grasped his head by his hair. As he moved his fingers she began to grind her ass into the bedsheets, crying out as his touch brought her to orgasm for the first time that night.

"Oh, Jesus," she gasped, breathing hard, "don't stop, please . . ."

Canyon bit both her nipples in turn, then moved his mouth down over her ribs, her belly, until he was able to remove his fingers and replace them with his mouth. He inhaled her scent, then ran his tongue over her, savoring her nectar.

"Oh, yes . . . Jesus, please don't stop . . . ooh, ooh, Canyon, you're killing me."

He slid his hands beneath her, cupped her buttocks in his big hands, and lifted her ass off the bed. This gave him easier access to her, and he used his tongue to lick every inch of her while she cried out and beat her fists on the bed.

"Ooh . . . yes, yes . . . Oh, God, yes . . . ahhh, Canyon."

She shuddered, and then almost screamed as in succession she experienced her second, third, and fourth orgasms of the night, each more intense than the one before it.

Canyon wasn't finished with her, though. He straddled her, and before the waves of sensation from her last orgasm had faded he pressed the head of his penis to her moist entryway and then punched it home. She gasped and convulsively lifted her legs and wrapped them around his waist. Once again he slid his hands under her to cup her buttocks and then began driving himself into her again . . . and again. . . .

All the while she was urging him on, her mouth right next to his ear.

"Oh, yes, yes . . . oh, please, Canyon . . . hard, Canyon . . . God, you're . . . you're crushing the life out of me . . . don't stop."

When she came again he felt her sharp teeth on his ear, and then he felt nothing else as he exploded into her . . .

"I think I need new ribs," she said later.

"I'm sorry," he said. "I think you bit off my ear."

"I'm sorry, too."

They both began to laugh. They were lying on their backs, the perspiration drying on their bodies, and she turned to him to kiss his shoulder.

"Oh, Canyon, that was so good—no, it was much better than good, it was . . . indescribable!"

"It was sort of nice," he said.

"Sort of?" she asked, trying to pinch some loose skin from his waist but not finding any. "It was as marvelous as I knew it would be from the moment I saw you."

"Right from the beginning?"

"When I opened the door and saw you standing in the hall," she said, "I immediately imagined you here, in my bed with me. Does that shock you?"

"No," he said, "it pleases me."

"How many women have told you that before?" she asked. "No, don't answer that. I don't want to know."

She slid her hand down over his belly and took hold of his penis.

"Sally," he said, "I really do need time—"

"Relax," she said, sliding down between his legs, "I'll do all the work . . . again."

* * *

"Where are you going?"

Sally had just woken up to see Canyon getting dressed.

"I have to go to my room," he said, pulling on his boots. "I don't want the Senator to see me coming out of yours in the morning."

"He won't care."

"You wouldn't get fired?"

"He couldn't get along without me," she said, setting her chin down in both hands. She was lying on her belly and he admired the lines of her back, the rise of her buttocks.

"Well, I have some work to do," he said. "I was having some papers delivered to the hotel. I want to go down to the desk and check—"

"Work," she said. "Terrible." She turned over onto her back and let her head hang down off the bed. Her big, beautiful breasts flattened out on her chest. "Don't go downstairs. The desk has instructions to slide deliveries under the door, or leave them outside the door. Just check. Your work is probably there."

"Thanks, Sally."

He started for the door and she called, "Canyon?"

He turned and saw that she was sliding a hand down between her breasts, over her belly, and then nestling it between her legs.

"Are you sure you want to go?"

"I don't want to go, you little tease," he said, walking back to the bed, "but I have to."

He leaned over and kissed both of her breasts. She took her hand from between her legs and brought it up to his face. Her fingers were wet and he took them in his mouth and sucked her nectar from them.

"I'll see you later," he said, "for breakfast."

"Pooh," she said, "go ahead and leave."

As he went out the door he knew from her tone that she didn't mean it at all. He'd meant what he had said, though.

He didn't want to leave, but he had to see if those files had been delivered so he could go over them tonight.

He went to the front door of the suite, opened it, and saw an envelope on the floor. It had been too thick to slide beneath the door. He picked it up and headed for his room. En route he saw Senator Brown walking toward him, probably coming from his office.

"Working late, Senator?"

Harrison Brown looked up, startled at Canyon's appearance, or simply startled from some reverie.

"O'Grady," he said. "What? Am I working late? I'm not working late, my good man, I'm just always working."

"I see."

"I hope you and Miss Cole got . . . properly acquainted," the Senator said. Canyon studied the man closely to see if he meant more than just the words he was saying.

"We had a very pleasant dinner, sir."

"Good, good," the Senator said, "Are you turning in for the evening?"

"I thought I would, sir, yes."

"I'm going to have a glass of brandy. Would you care to join me?"

"That's very kind of you, Senator," Canyon said, "but I really do have some reading to do before I turn in for the night."

"I understand," Brown said. "We all have our work, don't we—but a glass of brandy can sometimes stimulate the mind, eh?"

Canyon didn't tell the Senator that he'd had all the stimulation he needed for one night. He also didn't relish the thought of sharing a glass of brandy with the man and discussing the pros and cons of slavery.

"I suppose it would, sir, but I really do have to get to work."

"I understand. I suppose I should respect a man who won't be swayed from his work. For some of us," Brown added, "our work is all we have."

"Good night, Senator."

For a moment Canyon thought the man hadn't heard him, but then the Senator looked at him and said, "Oh, yes, good night. See you in the morning."

Canyon watched Senator Brown walk toward his bedroom, then opened the door to his own room and went inside.

The room was plushly furnished, as were all the rooms in the suite. Canyon removed his boots and his jacket and sat in a velvet-covered armchair to go over the files on the first five murders.

6

At 6 A.M. the next morning a train pulled into the station in Washington, D.C., and a tall man got off, carrying a worn carpetbag. He looked both ways on the platform before proceeding to the street to find a cab.

"I need a cheap hotel," he told the driver.

"A flophouse?"

"Flophouse," the man said, never having heard the term before. "That sounds right."

"Get in," the driver said, picking up his reins. "There's one not far from here."

Within ten minutes the man had a room in a rundown hotel. He paid cash for one night, even though he had no intention of sleeping there.

In his room he dropped the carpetbag onto the bed, opened it, and reached inside. His hand came out holding a Navy Colt, a gun he was not that familiar with, but one he had practiced with a lot recently. That was a rule of the club. They never let you leave until you had practiced long and hard with one particular gun.

He held the gun out in front of him and sighted down the barrel. He cocked the hammer and squeezed the trigger. The hammer dropped with a click on the empty chamber.

The assassin was in Washington, and he was ready. Now all he had to do was wait.

Canyon woke early the next morning and went back to the files, once again settling into the comfortable armchair.

The chair had been so comfortable the previous night that he had almost fallen asleep in it.

He leafed through the papers in the file folders to reassure himself that what he had noticed the night before was still there. It was, and that, coupled with the fact that Senator Harrison Brown was a man of strong opinions, convinced Canyon that Abraham Lincoln had been correct in sending him to guard the Senator.

Harrison Brown was a prime candidate for assassination.

At breakfast—attended by both Senator Brown and Sally Cole—Canyon decided not to tell the Senator the conclusion he had come to. He preferred to let the man continue to resent his presence. He didn't want the Senator constantly looking over his shoulder for a gunman. That was Canyon's job. Very often a jumpy man was a hard man to protect, simply because you never knew which way he was going to jump.

When Canyon had come out for breakfast the table had been cleaned of the dinner debris, and breakfast had been laid out on another table. He had picked up a plate, piled it high with eggs, bacon, potatoes, and biscuits, and then joined Senator Brown.

"Good morning, Senator," he said, sitting down.

The Senator had obviously risen early, or perhaps had not even been to bed. Whichever the case, the older man was approaching the new day with a good appetite. He had almost as much food on his plate as Canyon had, and the fact that his portion was slightly smaller was probably because he had already eaten some of it.

"Good morning, O'Grady," the Senator said. "You have a good appetite, I see."

"You seem to do all right yourself, Senator."

"Breakfast is virtually the only meal of the day I give any attention to," Brown said. "Very often I am too busy to give the other meals any consideration. If you start the day with a good meal, you can go a long way."

"I agree," Canyon said. "Breakfast is one of my favorite meals."

A big man, Canyon had to keep his body well supplied with food, and he was so active that he had no problem maintaining the body Sally Cole had been so pleased with the night before.

Sally came in a few minutes after Canyon, bidding both men good morning. She came to the table with considerably less food than either of the men had taken.

"Did you sleep well, Canyon?" she asked.

"Very well, thank you . . . Sally."

Senator Brown showed no surprise at the fact that they were calling each other by their first names.

"Senator, what time is the speech you're going to be making?" Canyon asked.

"Three P.M."

"I had the impression it was supposed to be earlier," Canyon said.

"It was, but I rescheduled it," Senator Brown said. "I'll be meeting with the President—as I told you last night—and then making my statement in front of the White House."

"I see," Canyon said. "Before that you'll be meeting with some of your colleagues."

"That's correct," Senator Brown said. "It's all as we discussed last night, Mr. O'Grady."

"Yes, sir," Canyon said, "I'm just going over it again so that I know I have it straight."

According to the schedule, the only public appearance the Senator would be making was when he gave that statement in front of the White House. That would be the perfect time for an assassin to strike—and the big red-haired agent would be right there. Of course, the trick would be to keep the Senator *and* would-be assassin alive. That wasn't going to be an easy task, considering that these assassins obviously did not mean to be taken alive.

Going over the files the night before, Canyon had come

to the conclusion that all of these assassinations had to be connected, even though the assassins were different. The connection, then, had to be that these killers were being sent out to kill from the same place. The thought of assassins being dispatched from one point to different parts of the country to kill and then be killed was not a very comforting one.

It would be even less comforting when he told Wheeler and Lincoln his theory.

"Sally, I'll want you with me every step today," Senator Brown said.

"Yes, sir."

"Do you think that's such a good idea, Senator?" Canyon asked.

The Senator looked at Canyon and said, "I need my assistant with me today, Mr. O'Grady."

"Yes, sir, but if an attempt on your life is anticipated—"

"Anticipated by you, sir," the Senator reminded Canyon, "not me."

"I understand that, sir," Canyon said, "it's just that as long as there's a chance—"

"I'm a politician, O'Grady," Harrison Brown said. "Miss Cole has worked for politicians before. She understands the risks involved."

"He's right," Sally said, "I do. I appreciate your concern, Canyon, but I work for the Senator, and I'll go where he needs me to be. That's my job."

"And she does it very well," the Senator said.

"I'm sure she does," Canyon said. He couldn't argue with both of them. Maybe he could convince Sally when he got her alone.

"Is everyone finished with breakfast?" Brown asked, standing up. He didn't wait for an answer. "I'll get my things from my office and we'll be on our way."

Canyon waited until he was sure the Senator was out of earshot, and then he leaned forward and said, "Sally, I'm convinced that there is a good chance that someone will try to assassinate the Senator."

"As he said, Canyon, there are risks involved in political life, in his business."

"I know that," Canyon said, "but there's no reason for you to be exposed to danger."

"We've gone over this already—"

"At least stay here today," he said.

"Can you guarantee that the attempt will happen today?" she asked.

"Of course not—"

"Then it's settled," she said, standing. "I have to collect some things, too."

She was stubborn—but then most of the women Canyon O'Grady was attracted to were.

No, he couldn't guarantee that the assassination attempt would be today, but if the killing of the actor was a rehearsal for this, no one would expect another attempt so soon.

The more he thought about it, the more convinced he became that today would be the day.

The assassin checked out of his hotel at 2 P.M. He paid his bill, ignoring the disdainful look the desk clerk was giving him. He would have liked to wipe the look off the man's face permanently, but that would have attracted unwanted attention. That was something else the club taught you.

After he had checked out, he left the hotel and waved down a cab.

"Where do you want to go?" the driver asked.

"Just drive around for a while," the assassin said.

"You don't want to go nowhere?"

"I do," the assassin said, "but not right now. Just drive around. I'll tell you where to take me when the time is right."

The driver shrugged, figured he had a strange one, and also figured that his money was as good as any sane person's. If the fella just wanted to drive around, then that's what they'd do.

It wasn't until the killer was gone from the hotel and out

of reach that the clerk realized that the man had not turned in his room key.

Canyon O'Grady dutifully followed Senator Brown around Washington while the Senator went about his business. Canyon really hadn't yet seen why the Senator wanted his assistant with him, but he was through arguing that point with either of them.

There was a stop for lunch, but they all ate quickly and lightly because the Senator was in a hurry.

Finally they went to the White House for the Senator to meet with President Lincoln. Neither Canyon nor Sally was permitted to enter the Oval Office with the Senator, so they waited outside in the same spot where Canyon had waited the previous morning.

"You know," Sally said, "in all the time I've worked in Washington, this is the first time I've ever been inside the White House. It's exciting."

"Yes, it is."

She looked at him. "You've been here many times before, haven't you?"

"Well," he said, "as a matter of fact I was in this very spot yesterday morning."

"I knew it," she said. "You get around, Canyon O'Grady." She leaned closer and said, "I almost came to your room last night."

"Why didn't you?"

She sat back and said, "I remembered what you said about having to work. Besides, when I opened my door I saw the Senator."

"Aha," Canyon said, "almost got caught, huh?"

"I fell asleep after that," she said. "You wore me out."

"*I* wore *you* out?"

"Shhh," Sally said as the woman sitting at the desk outside the Oval Office door looked their way.

Canyon leaned closer to Sally and whispered, "Wouldn't you like to make love right here?"

"That would be exciting, wouldn't it?" Sally said. They were leaning closer together like coconspirators, and the smell of her hair and skin filled his nostrils.

"What will happen after today, Canyon?" she asked.

"That depends on what happens today," he said.

"If there's no attempt on the Senator's life?"

"Then I guess I'll be spending another night in the suite."

"And if there is an attempt?"

"Hopefully I will have caught the would-be assassin, and this part of my job would be done."

"And we would never see each other again," she said sadly.

"That's not necessarily true, Sally," he said. "We'll see each other whenever you're in town and whenever I'm in town."

"Whenever we're both not too busy," she added. "As I said, Canyon, we'll never see each other again."

At that moment the door to the Oval Office opened and both Senator Brown and President Lincoln appeared.

"I'm sorry we can't get together on this issue, Harrison," the President said.

"We can, Mr. President," Senator Brown said, "only if you change your way of thinking."

"I can't do that, Senator."

"Then we obviously have nothing left to talk about, Mr. President."

"I wish that wasn't so, Senator."

Senator Brown looked at Sally and said, "Come along, Miss Cole." He then looked at Canyon and added, "I suppose you had better come as well."

The Senator strode off with Sally Cole trotting to keep up with him. Canyon exchanged glances with the President and then hurried after the Senator himself. He would have liked to speak with the President, but his job was far from over where Senator Brown was concerned.

The scary part was about to start.

* * *

Outside the White House gates the slavery advocates were lining up to listen to what the Senator had to say. Fewer people were here than had been at the theater the other night to see Charles Henry Oliver, and there certainly were not as many women. It said something about the times that more people turned out to catch a glimpse of an actor than to listen to what a politician had to say. Then again, Canyon reflected, considering that most politicians spoke for a very long time, while saying very little, maybe that was understandable.

Of course, one person wasn't there to see him *or* listen to what Senator Harrison Brown had to say about slavery or any other subject.

He was there to kill him.

7

Canyon O'Grady caught up to Senator Brown before the man could reach the White House gates.

"Senator, do you mind if I go out first? I just want to check things out."

"Oh, all right," Senator Brown said. "I won't interfere with your job."

"Thank you."

"But don't interfere with mine," Brown said. "I won't wait too long."

"I understand, sir."

Canyon turned and walked to the White House gates. The soldier on guard there knew him and opened the gates for him. Outside he saw that about forty or fifty people had gathered, plus one policeman who stood with his hands behind his back. Most of the people present were men, and any one of them could have been there to do the Senator harm. There was no way, however, that Canyon could have obtained authority to search all of the assembled people, and even if he could have, just carrying a gun—many of the men did—didn't make you a would-be assassin.

Canyon surveyed the crown critically, then backed up until he was standing next to the soldier.

"Keep your eyes open," he said to the man, "there might be trouble."

"Yes, sir."

Canyon went back through the gates and said, "Ready when you are, Senator."

"I've been ready for some time, Mr. O'Grady," Senator Brown said, moving past Canyon to step through the gates. Canyon moved right behind him, without giving Sally a chance to precede him.

This was no time to play the gentleman.

The assassin saw the Senator walk through the gates and he drew his gun from his belt. He was not even going to give the man the chance to speak. As he brought the gun up another man backed into him abruptly and turned to complain.

"What the hell," the man said, "watch where you're—hay, whataya doin' with that gun?"

A couple of other men saw the gun and started to yell.

Canyon heard the commotion and shouted to the Senator, "Down!" and pushed the man to the ground just as a shot was fired.

The assassin had pushed his way through the assembled people, most of whom were now trying to get out of his way anyway. He had rushed his first shot, had fired just as the big red-haired man pushed the Senator to the ground.

The policeman pulled his gun, and the soldier took his rifle from his shoulder, but Canyon shouted, "Don't shoot. You'll hit someone in the crowd!"

He grabbed the soldier's arm and pulled him closer.

"Get the Senator to safety," he said urgently.

The assassin stood with his legs spread and pointed his gun again. This time when he pulled the trigger his bullet found flesh and someone cried out.

"He's shot the Senator!" someone yelled.

"Canyon!" Sally Cole shouted.

"Sally, stay down," Canyon called back.

The assassin had fired two shots and did not know whether his target was alive or dead. He had no time for any more shots. He now had to make sure that he was not captured.

Canyon saw the look on the assassin's face and thought to himself that the man was going to kill himself rather than take another shot at the Senator. He didn't know how he knew, he just did.

"Stop him!" he shouted.

He ran toward the man, feeling helpless as the assassin lifted his gun and placed the barrel against his forehead. Canyon ran faster, and as the assassin's finger squeezed the trigger he reached out a desperate hand and managed just to catch the man's arm. The gun fired, and the bullet dug a furrow in the man's forehead, but did not penetrate.

The wound bled profusely, though, and as the would-be killer sank to the ground someone shouted, "He's dead, he's dead!"

People were running everywhere as Canyon leaned over the man and picked up his gun. He stood up and looked over to where the Senator had been standing. There was a crowd of people there now, and the agent knew that someone had been shot, he just couldn't tell who it was.

General Wheeler arrived at the hospital and bore down on Canyon, who was standing with Sally Cole.

"Jesus Christ," Wheeler said, "what happened? O'Grady, how's the Senator?"

"Relax, General," Canyon said. He took the man's arm and pulled him over into a corner. "The Senator is fine, he's unhurt."

"I heard something about two people being shot."

"They were," Canyon said, looking around to make sure no one else could hear them. "The soldier on the White House gate was shot and killed. He gave his life to save the Senator. The assassin was also shot, but he's alive."

"Who shot him?"

"He did," Canyon said. "He tried to shoot himself. I tried to stop him. We both partially succeeded."

Canyon was about to continue when he saw Police Lieutenant Rollo Dugan walking toward them.

"General, listen to me," Canyon said quickly. "As far

as anyone else is concerned the Senator is dead, and so is his killer. Do you understand?''

"No. Wha—"

"I'll explain later," Canyon said urgently. "Just go along with me."

Before Wheeler could say anything else Canyon turned to face Dugan.

"I heard what happened," Dugan said. "Is it true?"

"Lieutenant Dugan, meet Major General Wheeler."

"How do you do," Dugan said, then repeated to Canyon, "is it true?"

"Is what true?"

"Was Senator Brown killed?"

Canyon looked at Wheeler, then said to Dugan, "Yes, Lieutenant. The Senator is dead."

"Damn it," Dugan said. "And his killer?"

"Also dead."

"Did you kill him?"

"Yes."

"That's too bad," Dugan said. "We could have questioned him. Do you think this killing was related to the other one?"

"Oh, I doubt that," Canyon said. "They seem unrelated to me. I mean, what do an actor and a politician have in common?" He looked at Wheeler and said, "What do you think, General?"

"I, uh, well, I agree with you, O'Grady," Wheeler said. "Totally unrelated."

"You had a man on the scene, Lieutenant," Canyon said. "Why don't you talk to him?"

"I will," Dugan said. "Where is he?"

"He was here a minute ago," Canyon said, looking around.

"Well, I'll find him," Dugan mumbled. "Tough luck on this one, O'Grady, but we're, uh, we'll be working together, right?"

"Oh, definitely, Lieutenant," Canyon said. "Partners."

Dugan nodded, then turned and went off to find his police-man, whom Canyon himself had already sent home.

"What the hell was that all about?" Wheeler demanded. "Why are we telling the law that the Senator is dead?"

"We're telling the law, and we're telling the newspapers," Canyon said. "And eventually, whoever sent an assassin to kill the Senator will hear it as well."

A light dawned in Wheeler's eyes.

"And they'll think that they've succeeded."

"Correct."

"And that's why you're saying the killer's dead too. So they won't be afraid that he'll talk."

"Correct again," Canyon said. "All this will buy us some time, sir."

"Time that you had better put to good use, Canyon," Wheeler said.

"I intend to, sir."

"Wait," Wheeler said, "here comes the Lieutenant again."

"Now what?" Canyon said.

They both turned to face the policeman as he approached them.

"I forgot to tell you something before," Dugan said, shaking his head at his own forgetfulness.

"What's that?"

"The other killer," Dugan said, "the one who killed the actor? He's dead, too."

"What?" Wheeler said.

"Yeah, he's dead," Dugan said, looking at Wheeler, then at Canyon. "And do you know how he died?"

"I prefer not to guess, Lieutenant," Canyon said. "Why don't you tell us?"

"He swallowed his own tongue," Dugan said. "You know, I didn't know you could do that."

As Dugan turned and walked away Canyon looked at a shocked Wheeler and said, "Neither did I."

8

"Well, I have to admit it, O'Grady," Senator Brown said. "You were right . . . and you saved my life."

"It was that soldier shielding you with his body who saved your life, Senator," Canyon said.

"The poor man," Sally Cole said. "You should do something for his family, Senator."

"Yes, you're right, Sally," Senator Brown said. "Find out about his family for me, will you?"

"Yes, sir."

"Why don't you wait outside, Sally," Canyon said, "and I'll take you back to the hotel."

"All right."

Canyon waited until she had left the room before speaking to the Senator again. They were in a hospital room that Canyon had commandeered in order for the Senator to be secluded. He was, after all, supposed to be dead.

"Senator," Canyon said, "I'm going to need your cooperation."

"To do what?"

"In order for me to catch the people who are sending out these killers, I'll need you to be dead . . . for a while."

"What?"

"We're feeding the newspapers the story that you were killed today."

The Senator sat stunned for a moment, then said, "But my work—"

"Senator, this is only going to work if the country believes you are dead. I hope you can understand that."

"Well, of course, but—"

"Then you'll help me?"

"By being dead?" the Senator said dubiously.

"Yes, sir."

"For how long?"

Canyon hesitated, then said, "For however long it takes, sir."

The Senator scowled, then asked, "Do I have to stay here?"

"We can provide security for you here, sir."

The man's scowl deepened, then he looked at the bed in the room and said, "I hope that damned thing is comfortable."

Canyon smiled. "Thank you, sir."

He promised to have whatever the Senator needed brought to him and left the room. In the hall he found Sally seated on a bench, waiting for him patiently.

"Sally, I just have one more thing to do and then I'll take you back to the hotel."

She stood up and leaned closer to him to ask, "Is the Senator staying?"

"Yes," Canyon replied. "As far as anyone but us is concerned, he's dead."

She grabbed his arm, squeezing it tightly, and said, "Thank you for trusting me."

He smiled, patted her hand, then started down the hall. He really didn't have much choice but to trust her. She'd known before they arrived at the hospital that the Senator was unhurt.

He continued down the hall to a room that had a soldier on guard outside it. The soldier nodded at the red-haired agent and opened the door for him. Inside, the would-be assassin lay in a hospital bed with a doctor standing next to it. Canyon knew the man.

"Dr. Billings."

"Mr. O'Grady," the doctor said. "Is everything, er, arranged?"

"Yes," Canyon said. "Your hospital will be having a guest for a few days. I hope it won't be too great an inconvenience to you."

"Not when you consider the alternatives," the doctor said.

"How is this patient?"

"Still unconscious."

"But he's going to live."

"He should," Dr. Billings said, "unless there's an injury here we cannot detect."

"Such as?"

"Well, there could be a blood clot somewhere, but I don't think that's the case."

"Why is he still unconscious?"

"He took a nasty blow to the head with that bullet, Mr. O'Grady. The wound itself is not serious, but the shock that he's experienced will probably keep him unconscious for a while."

"How long is a while?"

The doctor, a young, good-looking man with narrow shoulders and small, almost effeminate hands, slid his hands into his smock pockets and said, "That is hard for me to say."

"Doctor, I really need to talk to this man."

"I realize that," the young doctor said, "and I wish there was something I could do, but I'm afraid all we can do is wait."

"Wait," Canyon repeated unhappily. "I guess there's not much else I can do."

He looked at the man in the bed and noticed that he was wearing a hospital gown.

"His clothes," he said.

"What?"

"Where are his clothes?"

"They're in that closet," the doctor said, pointing.

"Did you go through his pockets?" Canyon said, crossing the room to the closet.

"Of course not."

Canyon opened the closet and saw the man's shirt, jacket, and pants hanging up. He felt the man's shirt, squeezing the pockets, but they were empty. He did the same to the pants, but they also yielded nothing. Nor did the jacket pockets. He sighed and was about to close the door when he looked down at the floor. The man's boots were there, with his socks tucked into them. There was also a worn carpetbag on the floor. Canyon remembered the bag. It had been sitting in the middle of the street, and no one had even been sure it belonged to the killer except that no one else had claimed it, so it had been taken along.

He crouched down to rummage through the bag. There was an extra shirt, a pair of socks, a straight razor, and nothing else. Canyon suspected that the man had probably carried the gun in the bag until he reached Washington.

When Canyon closed the bag he heard something scrape. He picked it up and saw that there were a couple of other items on the floor underneath the bag. They had probably fallen from the pockets of the man's trousers. Canyon leaned over and picked them up, and found himself holding two keys. One key had a number stamped on it, but there was no indication of what it was for. The other key was attached to a flat piece of wood on which a hotel name was scratched. Canyon assumed that the first key was also from a hotel. Apparently the man in the bed did not believe in returning hotel keys. This habit—deliberate or not—had finally given Canyon O'Grady something to work with.

"Thank you, Doctor," Canyon said, closing the closet door. 'Someone will be in touch with you."

"Did you find something?" the doctor called after him, but Canyon O'Grady did not stop to answer.

He rejoined Sally and took her back to the hotel in a cab.

"Aren't you coming up?" she asked as he helped her out of the cab.

"I have a few things to do, Sally."

"Well, what about afterward?" she asked. "I mean, the Senator won't be here."

"Of course he won't," Canyon said. "He's dead."

"What I mean is I'll be all alone," she said. "In that big suite."

"And you'll be frightened?"

"Terrified."

"Well, if that's the case," he said, "I'll come back as soon as I finish my errands."

"Besides," she said, "we could talk about the Senator. I might be able to shed some light on who might want to have him killed."

"This is sounding like a better and better idea," Canyon said.

"I'll have dinner brought up for us."

"Fine."

Sally took a quick look around, then kissed him and headed into the hotel.

Well, at least tonight they wouldn't have to worry about the Senator hearing them, Canyon reflected.

He found the hotel he was looking for in a rundown section of Washington not far from the train station. It seemed the closer you got to the station, the worse the area.

He entered the hotel and approached the front desk.

"Yes, sir," the desk clerk said eagerly. "Got some fine rooms here, sir."

"I'm not looking for a room," Canyon said.

"Oh," the middle-aged clerk said, losing interest in him.

"As a matter of fact," the agent added, "I already have a key right here."

He set the key down on the desk and the man peered at it for a second before reacting.

"Hey!" The man grabbed for the key, but Canyon got it back first.

"What can you tell me about this key?" Canyon asked, letting the key sit on his palm.

"Well, for one thing it ain't yours," the man said. "Give it here."

"In a minute," the agent said, closing his fist around the key now. "Why don't you tell me who it does belong to first?"

"That's easy," the man said. "It belongs to this hotel."

"I know that," Canyon said patiently, "but tell me about the man who rented the room."

"He stole that key!"

Canyon, his patience wearing thin, had two choices. He could scare the man into answering his questions, or he could pay him to answer. He decided on the latter, and took a silver dollar out of his pocket.

"Now, why don't you answer my questions as I ask them?" he said.

Eyeing the dollar hungrily, the desk clerk said, "I thought that was what I was doing."

"Describe to me the man who rented this room."

His eyes still on the coin, the man accurately described the would-be killer of Senator Harrison Brown.

"When did he arrive?"

"Today," the man said. "This morning."

"And when did he check out?"

"Today, this afternoon."

"He didn't spend even one night?"

"No, he came in the morning and left in the afternoon, and then he left without givin' back the key."

That meant that the man had just arrived that morning, coming into town almost just in time to do what he had to do.

"What name did he register under?"

With a smirk the clerk said, "Smith."

"Tell me, do you know where the man came from?"

"No," the clerk said, "but I'd guess the train station."

"Why would you guess that?"

"I saw him get out of Charlie Moonshine's cab," the clerk said. "Charlie hangs around the train station looking for fares."

"I see," Canyon said. "Do you think I could find Charlie there now? At the station?"

"You sure could."

"Describe Charlie to me."

The clerk described a tall, dark-haired man in his early twenties, with hands—he said—like hams. "They're even the color of hams."

"All right," Canyon said. "You describe people very well."

"I see a lot of people," the clerk said. "Are we finished?"

"Sure, we're finished," Canyon said, flipping the coin into the air. The clerk caught it deftly and pocketed it swiftly.

Canyon turned to walk away and the man said, "Hey, how about he key?"

"I want to take a look at the room," Canyon said. "I'll return the key on my way out."

He went upstairs and used the key to get into room six. The room was empty except for a worn bed and an even older chest of drawers. He looked in the drawers, even though he expected to find nothing.

If the man had come from the train station, that would mean that he had gotten off a train. If he'd done that, he must have had a return ticket somewhere, and there was none in the carpetbag. Canyon cursed himself for not checking the pockets of the man's pants and jacket more thoroughly. He had merely felt them for something solid. He would have to go back to the hospital to check and see if there was a train ticket in any of them. Of course, the man might have had a one-way fare, considering the fate of the other assassins. Still, there could be a ticket stub somewhere. A man who saved hotel keys might save ticket stubs, even if the saving was an unconscious thing.

He finished his search of the rooms, finding nothing, and

left. Downstairs he dropped the key off with the clerk, then left the hotel and headed for the train station to find Charlie Moonshine.

Canyon found that there were quite a few horse-drawn cabs waiting for fares at the train station, but thanks to the desk clerk's description he was able to pick out Charlie Moonshine fairly easily.

"Are you Charlie Moonshine?" he asked the man.

Moonshine looked down from his driver's seat and said, "Who wants to know?"

"My name is Canyon O'Grady."

"You want to go somewhere?"

"I want to ask you a few questions."

The man shook his head. "Answering your questions could cost me a fare."

"I'll pay you for your time."

Charlie Moonshine smiled. "Start asking."

"You picked up a fare here this morning," Canyon said, and described the assassin.

"I remember him," Charlie said. "He wanted to go to a cheap hotel, so I took him to the cheapest one I knew."

"I know," Canyon said, "I just came from there. Do you know what train he got off of?"

"Mister, I meet so many trains. All you got to do is find out what trains came in this morning. I think I picked him up about six."

"I'll do that," Canyon said. "Can you tell me anything else about the man?"

"Can't tell you anything," the driver said. "He didn't talk except to ask for a cheap hotel. Sorry I can't tell you more. Why are you lookin' for this fella?"

Canyon handed the man a dollar and said, "Thanks for your help."

From there Canyon went into the railroad station and found out from the ticket clerk that at 6 A.M. a train had arrived in from Chicago. Knowing that, however, didn't make it a certainty that the killer had gotten off the train. It was likely, and probable, but it wasn't a certainty. For that he needed to find a ticket stub somewhere.

He left the train station and headed back to the hospital. In fact, he had Charlie Moonshine take him there.

When he entered the would-be killer's hospital room again he found no one in attendance.

"Where's the doctor?" he asked the guard, backing out of the room.

"He's in and out, sir."

"Has the man awakened at all?"

"Not that I know of."

Canyon nodded, thanked the man, and went back into the room.

He walked immediately to the closet and opened it. This time he put his hands into all of the man's pockets and was rewarded when he withdrew a ticket stub from the right-hand jacket pocket. A close look showed it to be the stub of a ticket from Chicago to Washington.

9

Canyon O'Grady had one more stop before returning to the Washington Plaza. He went to the small theater on K Street to talk with Harry Barlow.

He waited in Barlow's dressing room for the man to finish his performance. When Barlow walked in he did not look surprised to see Canyon there. He removed his black tie and sat down in front of his dressing-table mirror.

"Did you see the man today?" Canyon asked.

"I saw him."

"What conclusion did you come to?"

Barlow stopped removing grease paint and turned to face Canyon.

"This man is a very interesting case," Barlow said. "I was only with him a short time, but he appeared to me to be in a stupor."

"What does that have to do with hypnotism?"

"Nothing," Barlow said. "In point of fact, Mr. O'Grady, your man was not hypnotized."

"He wasn't hypnotized?" Canyon asked, surprised. "Then why won't he talk to anyone? I mean, I've seen criminals refuse to talk before, but at some point they usually break. This man did not seem to me to have a breaking point."

"Very astute of you, Mr. O'Grady."

"Just call me Canyon."

"Very well, Canyon. I agree with you. I don't think he has a breaking point."

"Then what was it that made him that way, if not hypnosis?"

Barlow considered the question for a moment, absently wiping paint from his face.

"If I had to choose one word, I would say the man seemed 'conditioned.' "

"Conditioned," Canyon repeated, frowning. "What exactly is the difference between being conditioned and being hypnotized?"

"Well, to put it simply, when I hypnotize someone I can get him to do things he would not ordinarily do. I cannot, however, force a person who is under hypnosis to kill someone."

"And someone who is conditioned could kill someone?" Canyon asked.

"When you condition someone that person is doing things almost by reflex. That person has been trained to do something—only one thing, usually—and he does it of his own free will."

"They kill others, and themselves, of their own free will? How? Why?"

"Because they have been conditioned to believe that it is the right thing to do."

Canyon considered what Barlow had been telling him, then nodded. "I think I understand what you mean. So then you wouldn't be surprised if I told you that shortly after you saw him today, that man killed himself?"

"Not at all," Barlow said. "If he tried to kill someone else, there's no reason why he couldn't kill himself as well."

"So let me get this straight—in hypnosis you are compelled to do something, while in conditioning you are trained to do something. Have I got it straight?"

"As straight as it can be in those terms."

Canyon nodded again and stood up. He extended his hand to the hypnotist, who stood up and took it.

"Thank you for your help, Mr. Barlow."

"Call me Harry," Barlow said. "Listen, I'll be performing here another two weeks. I'll leave your name at the box office and you have a free pass any night you want. Bring a lady.''

''I appreciate that,'' Canyon said. ''I'll be leaving town for a while, but if I get back before your run is over, I'll try to make it.''

Canyon walked to the door and as he opened it Barlow called out his name.

''Did that man in fact kill himself?''

''Yes, he did.''

''How did he do it?''

''He swallowed his tongue.''

Barlow grimaced and said, ''I didn't know you could do that.''

Going out the door, Canyon commented once more, ''Neither did I.''

By the time Canyon returned to the Washington Plaza it had been dark for some time. When Sally opened the door in response to his knock, he caught his breath. Her hair—which had been in a bun all day—was down, falling freely about her bare shoulders. Her shoulders were bare because she was wearing a dress that was daringly low-cut, revealing the tops of her firm breasts and the deep cleavage between them.

''I'm sorry I'm so late,'' he said.

''That's all right,'' she said. ''As long as you're here.'' She reached for his hand and drew him into the suite. ''The waiter and I have been talking about the weather.''

''You look . . . astonishing!'' he said.

''Thank you. Come, I think dinner is still warm—just barely.''

Tonight she had ordered a succulent side of beef with gravy, vegetables, and biscuits, and for dessert, fresh fruit. There was a bottle of wine in an ice bucket by the table, and as they entered the room the waiter grabbed the bottle and proceeded to open it. It was the same waiter who had served them at dinner the night before.

When the wine had been poured Canyon tucked a folded bill into the waiter's pocket and said, "I think we can take care of the rest of it ourselves tonight."

The waiter was white-haired and in his sixties, and had obviously been doing his job for a long time.

"As you wish, sir," he said with a short bow. "I will have someone come up in the morning to clean up and set out breakfast."

"Thank you."

He held both of their chairs for them, and when they were seated he let himself out.

As they started to eat Sally said, "Tell me what you've done since leaving me here."

Since she knew that the Senator was actually alive, he didn't see any reason not to tell her about Chicago and about his hypnotism theory being debunked.

"When will you be leaving?" she asked him.

"In the morning, I think. I'll have to see General Wheeler first, of course, and he'll report to the President. After that, barring any objection from either of them, I'll head for Chicago."

"About your theory," she said. "It doesn't sound so very different to me—I mean that these killers are being conditioned rather than hypnotized. I think basically you were right about the whole thing. You simply used the wrong word. You can't be faulted for that."

"Maybe not," he said. "Perhaps you're right."

"Of course I am," she said, and then giggled.

"What was that for?" he asked.

"Oh, I was just wondering what Senator Brown was eating tonight while we're sitting here having this feast at his expense."

That struck Canyon as funny also, and they laughed together.

"He's probably cursing out the hospital food," he said, and they laughed again.

"And the hospital bed, too," she added, eyeing Canyon

across the table. "Of course, we won't have that problem, will we?"

"I guess not," he said. "We have a lot of beds to choose from in this suite."

"Well," she said, standing up and coming to his side of the table, "why don't we go and choose one?"

She extended her hand and Canyon got up and took it. He allowed her to pick out a bed.

She picked hers.

He had Sally's splendid breasts in his hands, thumbing the nipples while she rode him with abandon. Her head was thrown back, her blonde hair hanging behind her. She was moaning aloud, once in a while saying words that only she could understand because they ran together so fast. All he could ever understand was, "Oh, oh, oh . . ." and "Yes, yes, yes . . ."

Canyon couldn't get enough of her firm breasts in his hands, squeezing them, kneading them, pulling her down at one point so he could suck her nipples.

She braced her hands on his chest so she could lift herself higher and come down on him harder. She was so wet he could feel her slick juices on his thighs, and when the air hit the wetness he felt cold. He didn't care, though. The coolness was a small price to pay for the other sensations he was experiencing.

Gripping her hips, he turned them over without losing contact, so that he was now on top. He drove himself into her as hard and as far as he could before withdrawing, and she gasped and reached out above her head to grasp the brass bedpost. She moved her butt, matching his tempo, biting her bottom lip and gasping every time their bodies came together. Finally they drove together and stayed that way, grinding against each other while they shared an orgasm that made the room spin.

She sighed and released the bedpost, licking her mouth

luxuriously like a cat who's just had some cream. He slid
from her and lay down next to her, feeling drained.

"That was incredible," she said. "My God, I've never
felt like this with anyone before."

"It was good, wasn't it?" he said, stretching his long body.

"Good?" she said, running her nails over his belly. "It
was special, Canyon . . . so special."

He didn't say anything, but closed his eyes while she
rubbed her hand over his belly.

"I'm sorry you have to leave tomorrow," she said.

"So am I."

"Of course," she went on, "since the Senator is officially
dead, you could take me with you."

He opened his eyes.

"Couldn't you?"

"Sally—"

"I know," she said, removing her hand from his belly
to run both hands over her own sleek body. He watched as
her hands moved up over her own breasts and then down
over her belly. "Let's sleep on it."

She turned her back to him and drew her knees up, getting
comfortable.

Sleep sounded pretty good just about now. Maybe when
they woke up she'd forget what she'd asked.

Peyton was in a panic. He'd heard from his contact, and
the Senator was not dead. He was going to have to do something before Talbot Lawrence found out, and he was going
to have to do it alone.

He still had time to save the club—and his own life. He
just wished he had another killer to send out to do it. This
was going to be a new experience for him.

Canyon woke abruptly, his eyes wide open and alert. He
didn't know exactly what had awakened him, but something
had. He held his breath and listened intently. He could hear

Sally's measured breathing, the beating of his own heart—
and a sound from outside their room.

He sat up in bed, took his gun from the night table, and
stood up, padding naked to the door of the bedroom. He
listened at the door for a moment, then tossed a glance back
at the bed. Sally was still sleeping in that curled-up position.
He turned the doorknob carefully, opened the door as quietly
as he could, and slipped out of the room.

Now he could hear clearly that there was someone in the
suite. From the sound of it, the intruder was in the front
portion, near the library and sitting room. It was just possible
that someone had come to kill him—or Sally—and didn't
know which room they were in. If that was the case, then
Canyon could simply stay where he was, in the darkened
hallway, and wait for whoever it was to come to him.

On the other hand, it was possible that the Senator had
rebelled against hospital food and beds and come back to
the suite. If that was the case, being caught naked and
creeping around was going to be embarrassing.

Still, better to be embarrassed—or em-"bare-assed"—than
dead.

Canyon decided that he would be better off getting it over
with and seeing just what the hell was going on. Maybe it
was just the waiter, come back to clean up.

Holding his Colt at the ready, up even with his shoulder
and pointed at the ceiling, he moved down the hallway. His
eyes were accustomed to the darkness, and he could see quite
well. When he reached the end of the hall he heard the sound,
someone bumping into something, and a man's voice
muttered, "Ouch, damn it!"

If this was an assassin, he was an amateur.

Canyon moved out into the sitting room and saw the
silhouette of a man.

"I wouldn't move if I was you," he said.

A pro would have frozen right then and there, but since
this was an amateur the man, startled, shouted, "What the

hell—'' and started firing his gun into the dark. The muzzle flashes lit the room, and Canyon threw himself to one side, knocking over a chair, and returned fire. With no time to be fancy, every shot he fired was meant to kill.

Carl Peyton couldn't believe it when the chunks of hot lead invaded his body. He couldn't be dying. He sent people out to kill others. This wasn't right. This . . . wasn't . . . right. . . . .

''Canyon!'' Sally shouted from another room.

Canyon didn't answer. In the darkness he moved to the fallen man and checked him for signs of life. Finding none, he stood up and looked around for a lamp to light. Before he could find one, however, Sally came into the room carrying one in her left hand. Her right hand was out of sight, something which did not escape Canyon's notice. She was also as naked as he, and the light and shadows were doing marvelous things to her body.

''Canyon, are you all right?''

''I'm fine,'' he said, ''but this fella is out of luck.''

''Who is he?'' she asked, not bothering to try to take a look.

''Well, he isn't someone who wandered into the wrong room, that's for sure.''

''A sneak thief?'' she asked.

''That's possible,'' Canyon said, ''but coupled with everything else that's been happening, that would be a coincidence, and I don't believe in coincidences.''

''What, then?''

''Come on, Sally,'' Canyon said. ''This fella was here to kill me, after which he was probably going to go to the hospital and make a try for the Senator. He must have been fairly desperate to try it, too.''

''Why do you say that?'' she asked.

''Because he was so bad at it. He made too much noise, and he fired wildly. He was definitely a man who had others do his killing for him. For him to try this, he must have figured he'd have help on the inside.''

"Me?"

"You," Canyon said. "How else would he know to come here? How else would he know that the Senator is still alive?"

"What makes you so sure that he did know?"

"He wouldn't have to try this, Sally, if the Senator was dead. What I can't understand is, if you were in place the whole time, why didn't you just kill the Senator?"

She didn't answer, but her other hand came into view now from behind her back, holding a gun. That didn't surprise him. He wondered if she realized that he was still holding his gun. Maybe she didn't care. Maybe she was reacting to her conditioning.

"Sally," Canyon said, "what do we do now?"

"I don't know about you," she said, "but I'll do what's good for the club."

"The club?" he asked. "What club?"

"I'm sorry, Canyon," she said, ignoring the question. "I really meant it when I said it had never been like that with anyone but you!"

He threw himself aside just as she fired, and this time he fired only once. The bullet struck her between her splendid breasts, and she fell back without a sound, dropping the lamp.

He went to her and looked down. The lamp had not broken, but lying on its side it was throwing off light at an angle. A shaft of light was across her face, and he could see that her eyes were open.

"Sally . . ." he said, kneeling beside her.

"Don't think you've won, Canyon," she whispered. "The club will send more, many more."

"Sally, what club?" he asked. He was about to repeat the question when he saw that it was no use. He would be asking the question of a dead woman.

Quickly he went to her room, got dressed, and left the suite. From all appearances it would look as if a thief had entered the room and they had killed each other. That wouldn't fool the police for long, though, not when they examined the guns. By then, however, Canyon would be on a train to Chicago, leaving General Wheeler behind to clean up his mess.

He had to find out what this club was that Sally had talked about.

10

Canyon O'Grady looked again at the key he held in his hand. It could simply be the key to another hotel room registered to a man using the name "Smith" or it could be the key to this club Sally Cole had mentioned.

Canyon had been in Chicago for two days now and was no closer to answers than he'd been when he arrived.

He stared out his hotel window at Michigan Avenue and thought back to his last day in Washington. . . .

"What a mess," General Wheeler said.

"It is a mess," Canyon replied, "and one that will have to be cleaned up."

"Oh, I'll have it cleaned up," Wheeler said impatiently. "I'm wondering if a trip to Chicago is really what's required here."

"General," Canyon said, "a stub from a railway ticket from Chicago to Washington is all we have to go on—that and this key I found among the latest assassin's belongings."

"Yes, but what has Chicago to do with murders committed in Washington?"

"There have been murders in other states as well, sir," Canyon reminded his superior. "Let me show you what I thought of on the way over here."

Canyon got up and walked to the map of the United States hanging on the wall. He also grabbed a pencil from the General's desk. He looked around for something with which to draw straight lines and finally grabbed a book. He drew straight lines to and from all the points where assassinations had taken place, including Washington.

"Do you see the lines, sir?" he said.

"Of course I can see the blasted lines."

"See where they intersect, sir?"

Wheeler got up from his desk and walked to the map. Canyon had drawn a dark dot at the point where all the lines intersected.

"I'll be damned," the General said.

"Yes, sir," Canyon O'Grady said. "Chicago."

"Let me in on more of what's going on in your mind, Canyon."

"Well, sir," Canyon said, "I'm thinking about this club Sally Cole mentioned. Sir, I believe what we're talking about here is a killers' club."

"A what?"

"An organization which trains and then sends out assassins."

"Who then kill themselves?"

"Think about it, sir," Canyon said. "One assassin, one job, both the target and the killer are dead when it's over. No loose ends."

"By God," Wheeler said, "that's monstrous. How can they train men to kill and then be killed?"

"I don't think they're trained, exactly, sir," the agent said. "It's more like a conditioning."

"Conditioning?"

"Yes, sir."

Briefly, he explained what Harry Barlow had told him.

When he finished, Wheeler said, "Well, it would certainly seem that Chicago is the next logical stop. All right, then, get going. I'll take care of the mess in the hotel."

"See what you can find out about the man and about Sally Cole," Canyon said. "When I've arrived I'll send you a telegram telling you what hotel I'm in. You can send me any information there."

"What are you going to do when you get there? Go to the police?"

"No, sir. I know a man who works in Chicago. Name's Frank Nolan. He does investigations for money."

"Do you think that's wise?"

"He knows the city, General, better than I do. He's a little unorthodox, but I won't use him unless I have to." He reached into his pocket and took out the key. "If I can just find the lock that this fits into, I may have all the answers I need."

"Yes," General Wheeler said, "or a whole new set of questions. . . ."

Now, in his Chicago hotel room, Canyon O'Grady stared at the key in his hand and then closed his fist over it. Where was the door that it opened?

The man he had spoken to General Wheeler about, Frank Nolan, knew the city of Chicago as few people did. It looked as if Canyon was going to have no choice but to make use of that knowledge.

Canyon got up, moved away from the window, collected his hat, jacket, and gun, and left the hotel. Outside, he asked a cabdriver if he knew the way to the White Horse Inn.

"Inn?" the man replied, laughing derisively. "It ain't no inn you're lookin' for, sir, it's an out-and-out saloon. Sure, I know where it is. Fact is, I drink there myself on occasion."

"Well," Canyon said, climbing into the back of the cab, "take me there."

"Yes, sir," the driver said. "White Horse Inn it is."

The ride only took about fifteen minutes. They pulled up in front of a rundown establishment that boasted "cold beer, warm women and hot food."

"Thanks for the ride," Canyon said, paying the man.

Instead of taking his money and leaving, the driver dropped down from his perch and stood in front of Canyon. He was in his late thirties, dark-haired, and stood no more than five foot four. The fact that he was rather rotund made him seem even shorter.

"You just get into town?"

"A couple of days ago."

"Well, if you need anything, if you need to find the best food or the best women in Chicago, you let me know, because to tell you the truth, you ain't gonna find either one here."

"I'm not looking for either one," Canyon told the man. "I'm looking for Frank Nolan."

"Nolan?" the man said. "Well, in that case, you came to the right place. This is his office! You see ol' Frank you tell him Blinky brung ya."

"Blinky?"

With a broad grin the little man said, "That's me," and then, nimbly as a monkey, he climbed back aboard his cab and shook the reins to get his horse going.

Canyon shook his head and went inside the White Horse Inn. The place really didn't differ very much from the many saloons he had been in from New York to San Francisco. The key word, of course, was "saloon." He'd been to many restaurants and gambling halls in other cities that put this place to shame, but when judged side by side with a saloon in Caldwell, Kansas, or Sante Fe, New Mexico, or Billings, Montana, the White Horse Inn offered the same things and had the same feel.

He attracted attention when he entered. He was big and red-haired, but the truth of the matter was that any stranger would have attracted attention. The place very likely catered to a large repeat clientele, and its customers were curious anytime a stranger walked in.

Of course, the men and women were curious for different reasons. The men saw in him—or in any stranger—a potential adversary—perhaps him more so than most others. Canyon O'Grady moved with easy confidence and grace, and any man could tell just by looking at him that as an opponent he'd be formidable.

The women who worked in the place, though, saw something else entirely. They too noticed the confidence and grace, and that coupled with the fact that he was big and handsome made them see a man who was a potential adversary of another kind—a worthy opponent in that age-old battle for supremacy between men and women . . . in bed.

Canyon walked to the bar and found a space with no problem. It was afternoon, but not yet late enough for the place to be filled up. Still, it was late enough for two girls to be working, and they were standing together at the other end of the bar, sizing up the newcomer. They were also arguing over who would be the first to approach him.

"What'll ya have?" the bored bartender asked. He was a florid-faced man in his early forties with a huge belly and forearms the size of railroad ties.

"Beer, preferably cold."

"It'll freeze your teeth," the bartender promised.

He drew the beer and placed the frosty mug in front of the agent, who gazed at it appreciatively. He lifted it to his mouth and drank half of the cold brew.

"I'm looking for Frank Nolan," he said.

"Ain't here," the bartender told him.

"Has he been in today yet?"

"I ain't seen Frank in a few days," the bartender said, "which is unusual. That means one of three things."

"And what are they?"

"He's either out of town, dead drunk somewhere, or just plain dead."

"I thought he got drunk here."

"He eats here and does business here, and has an occasional beer, but he never gets drunk here."

"Where does he get drunk?"

"Home."

"Where's that?"

The bartender shrugged. "I don't know, I ain't never been there."

"Who has?"

"Talk to the girls," the barkeep said. "They've gone home with him a time or two."

Canyon looked toward the end of the bar where the two saloon girls—or waitresses—were standing. Actually, they probably were more waitress than saloon girl. They weren't dressed as gaudily, or revealingly, as a saloon girl would be. They were, however, giving him the same looks he got from saloon girls.

"Thanks," Canyon said. He finished his beer and put the mug down. "I'll have another. Pour it out and I'll be right back."

The bartender shrugged and picked up the mug. "Don't blame me if it ain't still cold by the time you get to drinking it."

Canyon ignored the man and walked to the end of the bar where the two women were standing. He passed three or four men along the way, and they turned their heads to watch his progress.

The women were better than the place deserved. They were both in their early to mid twenties, and both were very pretty. One was blonde, with her hair worn up, reminding Canyon briefly of Sally Cole. He didn't need to be reminded of Sally. Killing her had been necessary, but it was something he had thought about quite a bit during the train ride from Washington.

The second woman had dark hair that hung down well below her shoulders. She was taller than the blonde, but the blonde was full-bodied while the dark-haired woman was slender. She also had darker skin than the blonde, and a small mole just to the right of her mouth that attracted the eye. It was that little extra something her face needed—along with her huge eyes—to make her the one he looked at when he spoke.

"Excuse me, ladies, but do either of you know Frank Nolan?"

"Frank?" the dark-haired one said. She and the blonde

exchanged a glance, and then she asked, "Are you looking to do business with Frank?"

"You might say that."

"And what else might we say?" the blonde asked.

"Frank and I are . . . acquaintances," Canyon said.

"Not friends?"

"If you know Frank," Canyon said, "you know that he has more acquaintances than friends."

They both grinned at that, and the dark-haired woman said, "Yeah, you know Frank. I'm Gina, and this is Liz."

"The bartender said that Frank hasn't been in for a few days."

"He's right," Gina said.

"Is that unusual?"

"Sure," Liz said.

"The bartender said Frank might be home, but I don't know where that is. He said that you girls have gone home with him a time or two."

"The bartender doesn't know what he's talking about," Gina said, throwing the man a glare. "We've walked Frank home when he's too drunk to walk himself."

Canyon decided not to tell them what the bartender had said about Frank Nolan's drinking habits. If they wanted Canyon to believe that they didn't go home with Frank and go to bed with him, that was fine with him.

"I'm sorry. That's just what I was told. Do you think one of you could help me out with this?"

They exchanged another glance now, and Gina answered cautiously, "We know where he lives, but we can't tell you."

"He'd be mad," Liz added, "no matter who it was we told."

"I understand," Canyon said, "but I need to know if he's in town. Could one of you help me out with this?"

"Well," Gina said, "I have a break coming up. I could go over to his room and see if he's there."

"I'd appreciate it."

She gave him a bold look then and said, "It will cost you, though."

"I'm willing to pay."

"She's not talking about money," Liz said.

Canyon smiled. "I know."

"Enjoy your beer," Gina said. "My break is coming up in about half an hour, and then I'll go and check."

"Thank you, ladies."

Canyon went back to his beer, nursed it as long as he could, then had another, all the while watching the room, which was watching him back. He also watched the girls work— bringing large trays of drinks to tables while dodging eager hands—and decided they were very good at what they did.

Finally, after he had ordered a fourth beer, still standing at the bar, Gina waved to him, indicating that she was going on her break.

Canyon had no idea how far away Nolan lived, but it couldn't be that far if she was going to walk there on her break. He expected her to be back within half an hour. That was why he was surprised when she came back through the door only five minutes later. From the panicky look on her face, what she had found in Nolan's room was not good.

"Mister," she said, grabbing Canyon's arm, "you better come quick."

"What's the matter?"

"Something's wrong," she said, tugging at him, "something is awful wrong."

11

As it turned out, Frank Nolan's room was upstairs from the White Horse Inn. It was remarkable, Canyon thought, that the bartender didn't know that, huh?

Canyon followed Gina around the side of the building to an alley and up a rickety flight of stairs. When they got to the top he saw that the flimsy front door to Frank's place was hanging off its hinges.

"Did you go inside?" Canyon asked.

"Y-yes," she said. "It's a mess."

Just because she had gone in and come out safely didn't mean there wasn't somebody still inside.

"Wait here," he said, taking out his gun.

He went inside, his gun held out in front of him. Nolan's lodgings consisted of only one room, and it wasn't very big, and it looked as if a cyclone had gone through it. Either that, or there had been a hell of a fight in here. Furniture was smashed, the bed was standing on three legs. Of course, the bed could have been that way before now. Still, it was fairly obvious that Frank Nolan had had some unwanted visitors. The question now was: where was he? And was he alive?

"You can come in," Canyon said, holstering his gun.

Gina came into the room very slowly.

"Do me a favor," Canyon said. "Tell me this room always looks like this."

"What?" she said, startled. "Uh, no, no, not like this. I mean, Frank's not neat, but it never looks like this."

Obviously she failed to see the humor in his remark.

"Gina, when was the last time you saw Frank?"

"Um . . . mister, could we get out of here?" She hugged her arms as if she was cold.

"Sure," he said. "Let's go."

He ushered her out the doorway and then did his best to put the door in place.

"I—I have to get back to work," she said when they came out of the alley.

"Just give me a minute of your time," Canyon said, taking hold of her arm gently. "When did you see him last, Gina?"

"Uh . . . three nights ago . . . I think."

"What about Liz? Would she have seen him after that?"

"I don't think so, but I can ask her."

"How many other girls work in the inn?"

"Two."

"Are they, uh, friends with Frank?"

She gave him a small smile and said, "Acquaintances."

He smiled back at her. "All right, suppose you ask Liz and the other girls. I'll come back here tonight and take you to dinner. How's that sound?"

"It sounds fine," she said. "I get off at ten, though."

"That's all right. I like having late dinner."

She shrugged. "All right, then. I'll see you tonight."

He watched as she walked to the front door, then thought of something.

"Gina?"

"Yes?"

"Does Frank have any real friends?"

"I only know one person who will admit that he and Frank are friends."

"Who's that?"

"A cabdriver named Blinky."

"I know Blinky," Canyon said. "I'll talk to him. Do you know where I can find him?"

"Anywhere there's a fare. Either that, or he'll be in tonight."

"Thanks, Gina. See you later."

"You better." She waved and went back inside.

Now all Canyon O'Grady had to go on was the cabdriver named Blinky. Hopefully, Blinky would know where Frank Nolan would go when he was in trouble.

Canyon preferred not to wait until Blinky showed up at the White Horse Inn later that night, so he went looking for him. Anywhere there was a fare, Gina had said. That probably meant the railroad station and hotels. Canyon went first to the station. Blinky wasn't there, but Canyon asked some of the other drivers where he might find him and came up with the names of a few hotels as possibilities. He found Blinky and his cab at the third one he tried.

"Blinky," he called, drawing the man's attention.

The little man frowned, then grinned and pointed down from his perch at Canyon.

"Hey, White Horse Inn, right?"

"That's right."

"Hey, did you find Frank?"

"That's what I want to talk to you about, Blinky," Canyon said. He looked around and spotted a saloon across the street. "Can I buy you a drink?"

"Sure," Blinky said, dropping to the ground. "I never turn down a free drink."

They walked across the street to the saloon, which was called the Shamrock. It was a couple of cuts above the White Horse. It was cleaner, smaller, and had waiters instead of waitresses so that none of the trouble that waitresses attracted would interfere with a quiet business.

Canyon got two beers from the bar and carried them to the table Blinky had already staked out. The cabdriver took a healthy swallow before speaking.

"What can I help you with, mister?"

"The name is O'Grady, Blinky, Canyon O'Grady. I'm looking for Frank."

"Yeah, I know that," Blinky said. "You didn't find him at the White Horse?"

"I didn't find him at the White Horse," Canyon said.

"Nobody there has seen him in three days, and his room is a mess."

Blinky grinned and said, "Frank's room is always a mess, Mr. O'Grady."

"Call me Canyon, Blinky," the agent said, "and I don't think it's usually this much of a mess. Not with broken and overturned furniture. It looks like there was one hell of a fight there."

"A fight?" Blinky said. He started to look concerned. "You mean you think something's happened to Frank?"

"That's the way it looks to me, Blinky," Canyon said. "Have you seen him in the last three days?"

Blinky frowned. "No. . . I think the last time I saw him was three days ago."

"How did he seem?"

"Well, he was working on something, I know that," Blinky said, "something he said was real important—but then Frank was always talking like that. Except . . ."

"Except what?"

"Well, I know Frank a long time, Mist—Canyon. I know when he's spinning a yarn and when he's telling the truth, and it seemed to me he was telling the truth. He really thought he was onto something big."

If Nolan was really onto something big, and he was alive and healthy, what were the chances he'd be able to help even if Canyon could find him? Maybe he should just stop looking for him and keep on working on this alone.

"He was real excited the last time I saw him," Blinky went on. "You know, real anxious, too, like he was also worried."

Canyon was growing distracted, preferring to deal with his own problem rather than with Frank Nolan's.

"Anxious, huh?"

"Yeah," Blinky said, "and he told me something that sounded funny."

"Like what?"

"He said the thing he was working on stretched all across the country, even to Washington, D.C."

The last part of the remark caught Canyon's attention again.

"To Washington?"

"That's what he said." Blinky nodded.

"And across the country," Canyon repeated, more to himself than to Blinky.

What were the chances that if some sort of assassination club was working out of Chicago Frank Nolan would run across it? Given Nolan's methods, and his usual area of expertise—the streets—maybe he *would* hear something, and maybe he'd get involved because it sounded like something big to him.

Canyon O'Grady hated coincidences, and hated to admit that they existed, but they did, and from time to time in his work he would run across one.

Maybe this was one of those times. Maybe Frank Nolan *was* working on the same thing he was, but from the other end.

"Mr. O'Grady?"

Canyon became aware that Blinky had called his name about three times.

"Yes?"

"If Frank's in trouble, are you gonna try to help him?" the little man asked.

"I'd like to, Blinky," Canyon said, "but don't get the wrong idea. I came here from Washington and somehow I think Frank and I may be working on the same thing."

"Geez," Blinky said, wide-eyed, "that's some coincidence, huh?"

Canyon O'Grady winced and said, "Yes, I was thinking the same thing."

"What do we do now?"

Canyon looked across the table at Blinky. "We?"

"Sure," Blinky said. "If Frank is in trouble, I wanna help."

"You can help, Blinky."

"How?"

"Assuming that Frank had a fight in his room with someone and got away, where would he go? I mean, if he was in trouble and had to hide, where would he go?"

Blinky frowned and said, "There's a few places he might go. I could check."

"Do that," Canyon said. "See if you can find him, and try to set up a meeting with me. Tell him what I told you, that I think we're working on the same thing."

"When I find Frank," Blinky said, "where do I find you?"

"I'm staying at the hotel on Michigan Avenue, the Spartan. Near where you picked me up today."

"I know the place. Hell, I know most of the hotels in town."

"That's right," Canyon said, "you would. Blinky, maybe you can help me right now."

"How?"

Canyon reached into his pocket and came out with the key he had been unable to identify. He put it on the table where Blinky could see it.

"Is this a hotel key?"

Blinky peered at it, poking at it with one pudgy finger.

"It sure looks like one."

"Do you know what hotel it's from?"

Blinky looked at Canyon. "Can I pick it up?"

"Of course."

Blinky picked up the key and examined it slowly, almost painfully.

"I might know," he said finally. "There's a few hotels it might be from. I can check it out for you."

"No," Canyon said, putting out his hand. Blinky gave him back the key. "You have to find Nolan. Tell me what hotels you think it might be from and I'll check them out."

"All right," Blinky said. The little man took a moment to think and then rattled off the names and locations of three hotels. Canyon quickly memorized them all.

"All right," he said. "We both have work to do, so we'd better both get started."

"Can I take you somewhere?" Blinky asked when they were outside.

"No," Canyon said, "I want you to get started. Find Frank and tell him I need to talk to him. I think it'll do both of us a lot of good."

"I'll tell him, Canyon."

He watched the little man climb back on top of his cab and thought that he had found himself an unlikely ally indeed.

12

Before checking out the three hotels Blinky had mentioned, Canyon went back to his own hotel to check for messages. The desk clerk handed him a telegram. He took it to his room and read it there.

It was from General Wheeler. Apparently the killer in the hospital had developed a high fever, and started talking in his delirium. He had said his name—Kenneth Grant—and they'd been able to check on him. He had once been a soldier in the army, but was drummed out for problems with excessive violence. The man Canyon had killed in the Senator's suite was named Carl Peyton. He, too, had once been a soldier, and he had also been kicked out. Canyon, refolding the flimsy piece of paper, had the beginnings of an idea, but he wanted to think it out further.

A check of his watch told him that he still had five hours before he was supposed to pick up Gina for dinner. That was plenty of time to take a look at the three hotels Blinky had given him.

He left his room and his hotel, that germ of an idea still growing in his mind.

When he showed the key to the clerk at the Dover Hotel he got an immediate reaction. It was the second of the three hotels Blinky had told him about. It was small, but several cuts above the one Canyon was staying in.

"Why, yes, sir," the clerk said, "that's our key, all right. Did you forget to return it when you checked out, sir?"

"I've never been here," Canyon said. "What happens when a key is missing?"

"We have a new one made," the clerk said. He was a slender man in his thirties, and his demeanor led Canyon to believe that he was more than just a desk clerk.

"Are you the manager?" he asked.

The man smiled and said a bit sadly, "I'm the assistant manager, sir."

"Do you change the lock on the room?"

"No, sir," the man said, "we don't go quite to that expense. If you don't mind my asking, sir, how did you come by the key if you've never been here?"

"I got it from a man in Washington."

"What was his name?"

"Why?" Canyon asked. "Would you recognize his name if I told you?"

"Well, sir, possibly."

Canyon frowned.

"But you asked me if it was my key. If you can't remember that you've never seen me here before, how would you remember the man's name?"

"Well . . . uh . . . perhaps it's an unusual name?" the man asked.

Canyon had intended to request a look at the register, but now he changed his mind. Something in the man's manner told him that wasn't going to be necessary. He already knew the killer's name from Wheeler's telegram message, and now he knew that the key came from the Dover Hotel. What he also knew—or felt—was that this man, the assistant manager, knew more than he was saying. To Canyon's way of thinking, the man was acting in a suspicious way. This feeling was supported by the man's reaction to Canyon's next question.

"What's your name?"

"My name?"

"Yes," Canyon said. "You do know your own name, don't you?"

"Well, of course . . . uh, my name is Walker, Dale Walker."

"Well, Mr. Walker, thanks for your assistance. You've been very helpful."

"I have?"

"Yes," Canyon said, "you have."

He turned to leave and Walker said, "Uh, sir?"

"Yes?"

"The key, please?"

"Oh, of course." Canyon tossed it to the man, who made an awkward grab and missed. The agent didn't see any reason not to give the key up. Physically, it was no longer vital to him.

"Thanks again," he said as Walker bent over to retrieve the key.

After Canyon O'Grady left, Dale Walker called over another man to watch the desk for him while he went into the manager's office. He knocked on the door, entered, and walked to the desk, placing the key on top of it.

"What's this?" the man behind the desk asked.

"A man just brought this key in, Mr. Myles."

Hammond Myles waited, and when nothing further was forthcoming he sighed and then said, "Don't make me have to drag it out of you bit by bit, Walker."

"He wasn't an old guest who forgot to give back the key," Walker said, "and he asked a lot of questions."

"What room is the key for?" the hotel manager asked.

"Two-oh-one."

"Did any of our people have that room?"

"Grant."

"And he kept the key?" Myles said in disbelief.

"It must have been an oversight."

The man behind the desk slammed his fist down on it. "Oversights are supposed to be conditioned out of these men. What did the fellow look like who brought the key in?"

"A big red-haired man."

"Not Frank Nolan?"

"No."

"Do we know where Nolan is yet?"

"Uh, no."

"I suppose letting him get away was just another oversight, eh, Walker?"

" That wasn't my fault—" Walker started to whine, but the manager cut him off with a motion of his hand.

"What was this red-haired man's name?"

"I, uh, don't know," Dale Walker said, looking down at the floor. He understood that not asking the man his name had indeed been another oversight.

"Jesus," the man behind the desk said, closing his eyes momentarily. "Didn't you ask?"

"No."

"I'll bet he asked your name, though, didn't he?"

"Y-yes."

"And you told him?"

"What was I supposed to do?"

"You were supposed to think, Walker, but then I can't blame you for failing to do that, can I?" To someone listening to the tone of the man's voice it would appear that he was being very understanding. "Thinking is not your strong point, is it?"

Dale Walker didn't answer.

"Is it, Walker?" the other man asked again.

"No . . . Mr. Myles."

"All right," Myles said, "go on about your business. I'll handle this."

"What about the red-haired man?"

"Well, we don't know his name, do we? Besides, I don't think we'll have any trouble finding him again. In fact, I think he'll find us. Now get out."

Walker started for the door and the other man called out, "And find Frank Nolan. At the moment he is more of a threat than some unknown red-haired man."

As Dale Walker left, the man behind the desk picked up

the key and stared at it. He was going to have to do something very drastic if he didn't want to end up the way Carl Peyton had in Washington.

He opened the top drawer of his desk and dropped the key into it.

Canyon O'Grady appeared at the White Horse Inn to pick up Gina an hour early and nursed a couple of beers while he waited, this time at a back table. The idea he had gotten while reading the General's telegram was still fermenting in his mind, as was the feeling he had about the assistant manager of the Dover Hotel—and the hotel itself.

What if the Dover Hotel was where the killers stayed before they went on their assignments? Was that why the assistant manager, Walker, was so nervous? If the hotel really was a stopover for assassins, then Kenneth Grant's apparently unconscious habit of pocketing hotel keys and forgetting to return them was going to play a big part in breaking up this assassins' ring.

A few minutes after ten Gina came to his table and announced, "I'm ready."

"Do you know a nice place for dinner?" he asked, standing up.

"I know a place that's nice," she said, "and expensive."

He smiled. "Good. Let's go. Do we need a ride?"

"No," she said, "the place I have in mind is not far from here."

"In this area?" he asked. "And it's expensive?"

"The area changes just a few blocks from here," she told him. "It becomes much nicer."

"Lead the way, then," he said. "I hope you're hungry."

"I'm starved."

They began to walk and he saw that she was right. The area changed drastically just a few blocks from the White Horse Inn. If they had been in a western plains town like Dodge City or Laredo, they would have crossed a red line between the good and bad sections of town.

The restaurant was called Allie's and was small but well furnished. The waiter took their orders which, on Gina's recommendation, were for steaks. She said that Allie's offered the best steak in Chicago.

While they waited she asked, "Have you found Frank yet?"

"No, but I'm working on it."

"What did you want to see him about, anyway?"

"I needed his help in something," he said. "I really can't talk about it, though."

"I'm sorry," she said, sitting back abruptly. "I'm too nosy sometimes."

"No," he said quickly, "that's all right. It's just not important for you to know, that's all. Did you talk to the other girls?"

"Yes. None of them have seen Frank since I did three days ago."

That didn't surprise Canyon, not with what he knew now.

"What about Blinky?" she asked.

"He hasn't seen him either," Canyon said, "but he's trying to find him now."

"Well, if anyone can it's Blinky. I don't know, but for some reason those two get along real well."

"Maybe they have a lot in common."

"I guess."

The waiter came with their steaks and Canyon only had to cut into his to know that Gina had been right. It was possibly the best steak he had ever eaten.

"You really know how to pick restaurants," he told her.

"I just wish I had the same luck picking men," she said, and then shook her head in self-reproach. "I'm sorry, I shouldn't have said that."

"It's all right."

"It's just that I've had a couple of bad experiences with men I thought were right for me," she said haltingly.

"Like Frank?"

"Oh, no," she said, her surprise sounding genuine. "Frank and I are just friends."

"And the other girls?"

"The same," she said. "We all really like him and try to look out for him."

"That's nice," Canyon said. "He sounds lucky to have all of you as friends."

"I don't know if he thinks of us as friends," she said with a shrug.

"Well, if he doesn't he's a fool," Canyon said, "because that's what you all sound like to me."

"Thanks," she answered. "I just wish one of us could help you now."

"You have helped me," he said. "I was hungry and you brought me here."

She smiled. "The pie's real good here, too."

"And the coffee?"

"Real good," she assured him.

"All right, then," he said, "let's have some."

After pie and coffee, outside in the street he asked, "How far do you live from here?"

"Not far. I can walk."

"I'll walk you."

"I'll be all right."

"I can't let you walk alone this late at night," he insisted.

"It's back in the other part of town," she warned him.

"All the more reason why I should walk you."

She smiled. "Thanks."

She lived at about the halfway point between Allie's and the White Horse Inn. Her room was similar to Nolan's, situated over a hardware store, with a stairway entrance in an alley.

"Here it is," she said.

"I'll walk you up."

They went up the stairs and he waited while she inserted

her key and opened the door. He was standing very close to her, so that when she turned she literally bumped into him. She was tall, which he liked, and he didn't have to lean over very far to kiss her. She was tentative at first, but then leaned into the kiss, which went on sweetly for some time.

"Would you like to come inside?" she asked.

He put his arm around her waist. "I'd love to come inside."

13

Gina had breasts like peaches. They were small and hard, but incredibly sweet. When Canyon caressed her nipples he could feel the blood rush into them, swelling them.

Canyon had taken the initiative with this young woman. Once they were in her room he undressed her slowly, feeling her catch her breath when he touched her breasts or her thighs. When she was naked he stepped back to look at her, and she stood shyly under his appraisal. Her breasts were high and small, her waist almost nonexistent, her hips slender, her thighs a bit too thin. The most pleasant surprise was her behind. It was high, round, and firm. He had thought that it would be flat, almost boyish.

He moved to her then and kissed her mouth, her chin, her neck, her smooth shoulders, her breasts and, finally, her nipples. She gasped when he took each of her nipples into his mouth, sucking them in turn.

He stepped back then, and she watched while he undressed. When his turgid penis came into view her eyes widened and she gasped. When he was totally naked he took her hand and led her to the bed.

Before she got into the bed she said, "Canyon, I have to tell you something first."

"What?" he asked gently. She had all the earmarks of a skittish colt or doe. If he made any sudden moves, she might try to run away.

"I know what men think about girls who work in saloons, but really, I'm very inexperienced. I mean I'm not a virgin, but I've only ever been with one man, and that was just—''

''Shh,'' he said, ''don't worry. It doesn't matter. You're going to be wonderful. I can tell.''

''Really?''

He sat down on the bed and said, ''Come on, sit down. That's the first step.''

She giggled and sat down next to him, saying, ''I thought taking off our clothes was the first step.''

He kissed her, cupping one of her breasts at the same time. That was when he first thought they reminded him of peaches.

''You have beautiful breasts,'' he said, kissing them. He lowered her to the bed on her back and continued to move his mouth on her breasts until she shuddered, a very tiny orgasm rippling through her body, like the ripples a pebble would have made when thrown into a pond.

When he kissed her belly she grew nervous. What was he going to do? When his kisses went lower still and moved down her pubic mound, she came close to swooning.

''Oh, my God,'' she gasped as his tongue fluttered over her entryway, ''what are you . . . ohhhh, I've never felt anything like . . . ohh, God . . .''

He slid his hands beneath her buttocks, cupped them, and lifted her off the bed so he would have full access to her. He squeezed her ass while he continued to kiss and lick her, and when he finally sucked her clit into his mouth she went wild. . . .

He allowed her to rest a little, not because she was tired, but just to let her absorb what had happened to her.

''My God,'' she said, ''I—I've never lost control of myself like that. I was like a wild animal.''

''Yes, you were,'' he said, smiling.

''I mean . . . I never thought a man could do that to a woman.''

"Not only can a man do it to a woman," he assured her, "but a woman can do it to a man as well."

She turned and looked at him, her eyes wide with wonder, like a child's.

"You mean . . . I could do that to you?"

"Sure you could."

She stared at him for a few moments, then looked down between his legs, where his penis still stood hard and ready. She reached down and touched him, closing her hand over him, and he moved his ass and moaned. Emboldened, she slid down so that her mouth was even with his crotch.

"You're so beautiful," she whispered, sliding her fingers up and down the length of him, examining him. "So hard . . . so smooth . . . so hot. Can I kiss it?"

"You can do whatever you like."

She leaned over and kissed the head of his penis, then stuck her tongue out and licked it. Bolder still, she leaned over and took the head into her mouth, sucking him the way he had sucked her.

"Mmmmm," she murmured, her mouth full, and let him slide free and said, "you taste so fine."

She opened her mouth and drew him inside again, this time taking more of him. She circled the base of his cock with her fingers and experimentally took more and more of him into her mouth, wetting him, setting him free and then taking him in again. After a while he touched her head, just to guide her, and she began to ride him with her mouth. He moaned appreciatively, then took her head in both hands and gently lifted it off him.

"What's wrong?" she asked. "Don't you like it?"

"Of course I like it," he said, "but we're just moments away from something happening, and I wanted to warn you."

"About what—oh," she said, then, understanding. "You mean—"

"Yes," he said, "and there are women who don't like the taste of it."

She stared at his penis, swollen even more now and pulsating.

"I couldn't imagine not liking the taste of you."

"Still," he said, "since we have all night. I have a suggestion to make."

She listened and then agreed to his suggestion, and took him in her mouth again. She started sucking him, her head bobbing up and down faster and faster, and when he knew he could wait no longer he reached to lift her from him just in time.

She watched in fascination as his penis erupted, white fluid actually shooting up from it again and again. She started to count the number of times he shot, and when she got to nine it trailed off.

His juice was all over his belly now, a pool of it in his navel, and she dipped the tips of her fingers into it delicately, then lifted her fingers to her mouth, licking them.

"Oh," she said, and dipped her fingers again, this time taking a little more, and thrusting her fingers into her mouth. She was like a child who has just discovered candy. He was going to ask her for a cloth to clean himself with, but by the time she finished with him he didn't need one anymore. It got to the point where she was licking his belly hungrily, and he felt his penis begin to respond again.

"Oooh," she said, looking at him, "more?"

"In time," he said, reaching for her. He brought her up beside him and began kissing her, his hands moving over her body, eliciting responses from her she never could have imagined. Finally, when his penis was fully erect and swollen again, he positioned himself between her legs and just let the head of it touch her moist portal. He rubbed himself up and down her slit, coming into contact with her clit, until she could finally stand no more.

"Oh, Canyon, please," she cried out, reaching for him, "please put it in me now! Oh, I can't wait . . . ooooh . . ."

He plunged into her without warning and she gasped and

moaned and lifted her slender legs up around his waist. She had told the truth, she wasn't a virgin, but given the amount of knowledge she had about sex, she wasn't very far from being one.

Of course, when this night was over, she truly would not be a virgin in any sense of the word.

When her orgasm hit her it was even more intense than before. She arched her back and raked his back with her nails, and then screamed when the first orgasm went right into a second one . . . and then a third. . . .

"Oh, my God," she said a little later, "I thought I was going to die . . . and I was so happy." She turned her head to look at him. "I don't think I've ever been as happy as I was when you were inside me."

"It wasn't like that for you before?"

"Before?" she said. "I've only ever been with one boy before, when I was younger, and all he ever did was punch himself inside me, rut like a pig, satisfy himself, and then leave." She looked at him and said, "This is the first time I've ever been with a man, and I never thought . . ."

"Thought what?" he prompted when she stopped.

"Well, I've heard the other girls talk about being with men—not that they're whores, or anything like that," she added quickly.

"I know."

"But they would talk, and I never heard any of them talk about a man who . . . who cared about their pleasure as much as his own, the way you did about mine."

"A man is a fool if he doesn't give as much pleasure as he gets, Gina."

She slid her hand down to take his and said, "Then I guess they've known a lot of fools. I'm really happy you're not one."

He lifted her hand and kissed it.

"Did you mean what you said before?" she asked softly.

"About what?"

She squeezed his hand with hers and ran her other hand over his chest.

"About us having all night?"

He smiled at her and said, "Oh, yeah, I meant it."

She slid one slender leg over him and said, "Good."

They made love twice more during the night, each time attacking each other hungrily. A new attitude toward sex had been awakened in Gina, and she embraced it openly. After a night with Canyon O'Grady, the young woman had no inhibitions where sex was concerned. She demonstrated this by waking Canyon in the morning by nuzzling him, her head down between his legs, her tongue very actively on his thighs, his testicles, and his penis.

"Haven't you had enough?" he asked.

She looked up at him from between his legs and said, "Never."

Thankfully, he was rising to the challenge, and when she brought her mouth down on him he was ready. . . .

Gina wanted them to have breakfast together, but Canyon told her that he had to go back to his hotel, get cleaned up, and start back to work again. She fell silent after that, and he knew what she was thinking. He'd gotten what he wanted, and now he was going to leave her and not come back.

"We can probably have dinner together," he said. "Will you be free if I come by at ten o'clock again?"

Her face brightened and she said, "I'll make sure I'm free."

"I'll see you later, then."

"You know," she said, "you never did tell me why you were in Chicago."

He kissed her, said, "I know," and left.

When he got back to his hotel he stopped at the desk for messages, hoping there would be one from Blinky, or better yet, from Frank Nolan. There were none.

He asked the clerk to have a bath drawn for him, then went to his room for fresh clothes. After he bathed and dressed he'd have a quick breakfast and then he'd get out there and find Blinky.

14

The manager of the Dover House looked up as his door opened. He prepared to reprimand whoever was bothering him, then snapped his mouth shut when he saw who was there.

"Mr. Lawrence," he said, standing up quickly.

"Sit down, Myles," Talbot Lawrence said.

Hammond Myles sat back down behind his desk as Lawrence seated himself in the straight-backed chair across from him.

"Tell me what's happening."

"Well, everything is going fine—"

Lawrence stopped him by lifting his hand.

"If you lie to me, Myles, you're obviously not the man for the job. I'll install someone else to manage this little way station."

"That won't be necessary," Myles said. "We've had some problems."

"Explain them to me."

First Myles told Lawrence the trouble Frank Nolan was causing them.

"How did he find out about the club?" Lawrence asked.

"The man is a denizen of the street, Mr. Lawrence. He knows almost everything that goes on in Chicago—or so I understand."

"Did you offer him money?"

"Well, no . . ."

"Don't tell me, let me guess. You tried to have him killed."

"Well . . ."

"I think you're getting carried away, Myles," Lawrence said. "Despite what our club stands for, it is not always best or easiest to kill your enemies. If the man was an annoyance, or even a problem, and if he lives as you say he does, he could have been bought off."

"I suppose you're right."

"Why, thank you," Lawrence said coldly.

"I'm sorry, I didn't mean to—"

"Never mind," Lawrence said impatiently. "What are you doing to find him?"

"I have men on the streets looking for him."

"This time when you find him, you'll have to kill him. Understand?"

"Yes, sir."

"All right. What's the other problem?"

Myles told Lawrence about the redheaded man who had returned Grant's room key.

"Grant is in the hospital in Washington," Lawrence said.

"My God," Myles said, "he's alive?"

"He managed to do his job, but yes, he's alive—for now. He's out of our reach, but he won't talk. What about this second man? Who is he?"

"We don't know," Myles said.

"Do you have men out looking for him?"

"No."

"Why not?"

"I feel he'll have to come back here," Myles said. "When he does, we'll be ready for him."

Lawrence regarded the man critically and then said, "Myles, that may be good thinking."

Hammond Myles wasn't sure whether or not he should feel complimented.

*   *   *

As soon as Canyon O'Grady stepped out of his hotel a horse-drawn cab pulled up in front.

"Need a ride, mister?" the driver called out.

Canyon looked up and saw Blinky looking down at him. He thought the man looked a little anxious.

"I sure do," he said.

"Hop in."

Canyon got into the back of Blinky's cab, and the man snapped his reins to start his horse and pull away from the hotel.

Canyon leaned out and called to Blinky, "Where are we going?"

"You want to see Frank, right?"

"Right!"

"That's where we're going."

Canyon didn't know what part of Chicago they ended up in, but they rode for more than half an hour before Blinky pulled the cab over to the side of the road and stopped his horse.

"Come on," the little man said, dropping down to the street.

"Why didn't you leave me a message at the hotel?" Canyon asked.

"Frank told me not to. He also told me to drive you around for a while before bringing you here, to make sure we weren't followed."

"Here" turned out to be what looked like an abandoned livery stable on a street of abandoned buildings.

"Let's go inside," Blinky said. He looked around, and then led the way into the building. Canyon took one last look around himself before following.

The inside of the building was dark, but Canyon knew someone was there because the place smelled inhabited. Someone had cooked something recently, and he could smell coffee brewing.

"Frank," Blinky called out hoarsely, "we're here."

There was no answer.

"Give him a minute to make sure we weren't followed," the little cabdriver told Canyon.

They waited about five minutes before they heard a rustle of movement, and then Frank Nolan appeared. His face looked somewhat bruised and battered, but other than that he seemed healthy enough. He was pretty much the way Canyon remembered him—still tall and lean and good-looking. His dark hair was now peppered with gray, even though he was probably not yet forty. His clothes looked old and lived in, as if he'd been sleeping in them for a few days.

"It *is* you," Nolan said to Canyon.

"It's me."

"I couldn't believe Blinky when he said you were looking for me. It's been years."

The two men had worked together some years back when they both had different jobs and different ideals.

Nolan approached Canyon and the two men shook hands. Then Nolan put a hand on Blinky's shoulder.

"Thanks for bringing him, Blinky. Now would you go out and stand watch?"

"Sure, Frank," Blinky said. He looked at Canyon. "I'll wait for you outside."

"Thanks, Blinky."

Canyon and Nolan waited until the little man had gone before speaking.

"Come on with me," Nolan said. "I've got some coffee on."

"I know," Canyon said, "I could smell it when I came in."

Nolan shrugged with a smile and said, "I know, but I need my coffee, even if I'm on the run."

Canyon followed Nolan to the back of the building and into a little room where a small fire was burning. On it was a coffeepot.

"It ain't much," Nolan said, "but while I'm trying to stay alive, it's home."

"Your friends have been worried about you."

"What friends?"

"Blinky, Gina, some of the other girls at the White Horse Inn."

"You getting to know Gina?" Nolan asked.

Canyon hesitated, then said, "She told me there was nothing between you."

"Hell, no, there ain't," Nolan said. "They're all nice kids, those girls. If you and Gina have got friendly, I've got no problem with that."

When they each held a cup of coffee Nolan said, "Now, why don't we start off by you telling me why you were looking for me, Canyon?"

"I need your help."

Nolan laughed. "Well, I don't know if I'm in a position to help anybody else, but keep talking."

Briefly, Canyon explained the situation to Nolan and described the events that had brought him from Washington to Chicago.

"And you think the Dover Hotel is a sort of stopover for these assassins on their way to their assignments?" Nolan asked.

"That's what I think. I also think, judging from what I've heard of your problem, that we may be working on the same thing."

"You're probably right," Nolan said, a look of wonder on his face. "Well, if that don't beat all. Ain't that a coincidence?"

Canyon winced, his usual reaction to that word.

"And how did you find me?"

"Well, Gina took me to your room when she saw what a mess it was, and Blinky did all the rest. He's a good friend of yours."

"Yeah, I suppose he is. Guess I should have told him where I was instead of making him find me himself, but I didn't want to get him involved."

"Suppose you tell me your story now."

"My story, huh?" Nolan said. "My story is I can't keep
to my own business."

"Tell me about it."

15

"I stumbled into it with my eyes closed," Frank Nolan said.

He had simply heard on the street that there were some strange comings and goings at the Dover Hotel. You can't shuffle men in and out of a hotel like that on a daily basis with none of them ever paying a bill.

"One of the desk clerks there asked about it, and got fired for his trouble. He was drinking at the inn one day when I was there, and he was complaining."

"He's lucky they didn't kill him."

"That would have attracted too much attention to the hotel."

"True."

"Anyway, that's how I heard about it, so I decided to look into it."

For a week or so Nolan had positioned himself in a doorway across from the Dover and verified for himself that there was something going on.

"The assistant manager always picks the men up at the hotel. The manager is always outside when the men arrive, and takes them in personally. How many hotel managers do you know who do that?"

"None."

"You're damned right. So somebody must have noticed me across the way, because the next thing I know there are two guys in my room trying to kill me. I got some bumps and bruises—and gave some—and got away. I been hiding out ever since, trying to figure out what to do.''

"So far,'' Canyon said, "there's nothing in your story that really proves that we're working on the same thing.''

"There's the hotel.''

"But we need more,'' Canyon said. "Is there anything you haven't told me? Something that those two men who tried to kill you might have said?''

"They said something about their club,'' Nolan said, thinking back.

"Think, Frank,'' Canyon said, "what exactly did they say?''

"They said I had to die for the good of the club. It was like they were sorry they had to kill me.''

"All right,'' Canyon said with feeling, "that clinches it, then.''

"The remark about the club?''

"Yes.''

"What is this club, anyway?''

"A killers' club, Frank,'' Canyon said. "They condition men to be assassins, then send them out to do one job. After that, the assassin always finds a way to either get himself killed or kill himself.''

"Jesus.''

"Is there anything else you know that might help us?'' Canyon asked.

"Just one thing,'' Nolan said after a moment. His face had lit up, as if he had just found the answer to something.

"What's that?''

Nolan smiled. "I know where they're training their men.''

"What?''

"Yeah,'' Nolan said, rubbing his hands together. "I went to the railroad station when the last three men arrived, and I found out where they had come from.''

"Where?''

"Denver,'' Nolan said.

"Well, that tells us where they're sending the men from, not necessarily where they're doing the conditioning, but you're right. It does give us our next step."

"Our next step?"

"Well, you can't stay here and hide indefinitely. Come with me to Denver and help me. I have a plan."

"A plan, huh?"

"Yep."

"Is this one of them plans where you come out alive and I come out dead?"

"No, nothing like that," Canyon said. "This is the kind of plan where you and I put the killers' club out of business. What do you say?"

Nolan thought a moment before answering.

"You know," he said finally, "I'm not noble or anything, not like you. I'm not always looking to do what's right. I mean, if I could have turned this into a lot of money, I believe they could have bought me off."

"Could have? Not anymore?"

"They tried to kill me," Nolan said, "and they sent me into hiding like a rat. Hell no, they can't buy me off anymore."

"Then we're going to Denver?"

"We're going to Denver."

"Good."

"But would you mind telling me your plan before we go? Just in case I don't like it, you understand."

After Canyon explained his plan they discussed when the best time to leave would be.

"After dark," Canyon said, "since they probably have men out looking for you."

"What about you?" Nolan said. "After you brought that key back don't you think they're looking for you, too?"

"I don't think so," Canyon said. "They're probably figuring I'll come back to the hotel at some point. My guess is they're waiting for me there."

"And you're not gonna show up."

"Right," Canyon said. "You stay here while Blinky and I get the train tickets. I'll get the latest train out, so we can transfer you to it in the dark."

"Uh, I don't have any money to put into this little job, you know?"

"Don't worry," Canyon said, "the government will pay for everything."

"In that case," Nolan said, "get us a private compartment."

"That's a good idea," Canyon said. "We'll be able to watch each other's backs easier that way. You do have a gun, don't you?"

"Of course I have a gun."

"Good," Canyon said, standing up. "Blinky and I will go to the station right now. You be standing by to leave at a minute's notice."

"But probably not until later tonight, right?"

"Right."

Nolan walked Canyon back out to the front of the building, but did not step outside.

"Be careful at the station," Nolan said. "They're probably watching there for me, but that don't mean they don't know what you look like."

"I'll be careful," Canyon said. "If it looks like they have too many men covering the station, I'll send Blinky in to buy the tickets."

"Just make sure the little guy knows the risks, huh? I don't want him getting killed and not knowing why."

"Frank," Canyon said, "I won't make him do anything he doesn't want to do."

"I say that all the time to women."

Canyon rolled his eyes and said, "I'll see you later. Is there anything I can get for you?"

"Yeah," Nolan said. "Speaking of women . . ."

Outside, Blinky asked Canyon, "So where are we headed now?"

"To the train station, Blinky."

"Hop in."

Canyon put his arm on Blinky's to keep him from climbing aboard just yet and said, "There are some risks involved here, Blinky."

"Tell me about them on the way," the smaller man said, and climbed into his driver's seat.

By the time they reached the station Blinky knew all of the risks involved, and he was still willing to help his friend Frank.

Canyon had Blinky stop his cab before they actually reached the station, and they walked the rest of the way.

"What do we do first?" Blinky asked.

"We've got to see how many men they've got watching the station," Canyon told him. "You take one side and I'll take the other. If you see someone you think is watching out for Frank, don't let him know you've noticed him. Just count heads and meet me back at the cab. Understand?"

"I understand."

"Don't take any chances."

"I understand," Blinky said again. "I ain't dumb, you know."

"All right, let's go."

Canyon O'Grady knew he was taking a big chance walking into the railroad station like this. If the men there had been given his description, he was going to have a devil of a time getting out alive. Still, he and Blinky had to know what they were dealing with, so he actually had no choice.

They walked into the station from their respective sides, and Canyon had to admire the little man's courage.

The men of the killers' club were not hard to spot. There were two lounging on Canyon's side of the station, eyes sweeping the area, bored looks on their faces. He was willing to bet that there were also two men on Blinky's side.

He had told Blinky not to take any chances, but he decided to take one himself. He purposely walked past one of the men. The man's gaze passed over him and then away, apparently without recognition. Evidently the watchers' bosses hadn't given them Canyon's description. Not wanting to confuse the issue, their bosses had probably simply told them to watch for Frank Nolan.

Canyon took the opportunity to approach the ticket cage and ask the clerk what the latest train out to Denver was.

"Got one leaving at nine tonight. Next one after that t'aint' 'til mornin'," the man said.

"That's fine," Canyon said. "I need two tickets and a private compartment."

"That'll be costly."

"I'll pay it," Canyon said.

The clerk tallied up the total and accepted the money from Canyon, handing him two tickets.

"If you ain't here on time, the train'll leave without you," the clerk warned.

"We'll be here."

Leaving the station, Canyon walked past the other watcher, who gave him the same bored, fleeting glance. If he'd had the makings of a cigarette, he would have stopped and asked the man for a match. It was just as well he didn't, because that would have been too playful, not to mention damned foolish.

Outside the station he walked at a normal pace to the cab and found Blinky waiting, anxiously shifting from one foot to the other. The little man took some quick steps to join Canyon as he reached the cab.

"Jesus," Blinky said, "I thought something happened to you. What took you so long?"

"I got the tickets."

"Already? When are you leaving?"

"Tonight," Canyon said, looking around to make sure they weren't being watched—or stalked. "Blinky, there were two men on my side of the station, and they didn't recognize me."

"Well, there was two on my side, just standing around staring into the air, and they sure as hell didn't know who I was."

"All right," Canyon said, "that's four, and we'll have to assume that there'll be at least that many even late at night."

"So how you gonna get Frank past four men?" Blinky asked.

"That's a good question, Blinky," Canyon O'Grady said, "that's a real good question."

16

"Where is he?" Gina asked.

They were sitting at a table in the White Horse Inn and Canyon had just told her that Frank Nolan was all right.

"I can't tell you that, Gina," Canyon said. "It's not that I don't trust you," he hastened to add, "but it's for your own safety."

"Why?"

"Some people are looking for him, Gina, and if they find him they're going to kill him."

"Why?" she asked again.

"I can't tell you that either," Canyon said. "In fact, I can't tell you very much. In fact, I can't have dinner with you tonight, because we're leaving."

"To go where?" she asked, and then she raised her hands and said, "Never mind. You can't tell me that either."

"That's right," Canyon said, "I just came to say good-bye."

"Will you ever come back?" she asked.

"Honestly don't know, Gina."

Gina stared at Canyon for a few moments, then turned her head and looked around the room.

"I guess I should get back to work."

"I guess so."

They both stood up, and Canyon leaned over awkwardly and kissed Gina on the cheek.

"Frank should be back soon, Gina."

"Good," she said, "good, we've missed him around here."

Canyon started for the door and Gina called out, "Ryder!"

"What?" he asked, turning.

"My last name," she said. "It's Ryder."

He smiled. " 'Bye, Gina Ryder."

As he went out the door she waved and said, mostly to herself, "Good-bye, Canyon O'Grady."

Blinky was waiting for Canyon outside the inn.

"Your hotel?" Blinky asked.

"No," Canyon said. "I don't have anything there that I can't do without. I don't want to go near it, just to play it safe."

"Where to, then?"

"First I want to send a telegram to Washington," Canyon said. "Then we have a few hours before we have to be at the railroad station. We might as well go and wait with Frank."

"Right."

"Let's pick up some food and coffee," Canyon said. "He might as well eat well on his last night in Chicago—for a while, anyway."

This time when Hammond Myles talked with Talbot Lawrence, it was Lawrence who was sitting behind the desk. Myles figured it was the other man's way of telling him who was really in charge.

"What is the situation?" Lawrence asked.

"We haven't located Nolan yet."

"Have you checked the railroad station?"

"We have men there."

"How many?"

"Four."

"Increase it to six."

"Yes . . . sir."

"And what about the other man?"

"We don't know where he is."

"I know that," Lawrence said. "Has he been seen near the hotel, again?"

"No . . . sir."

Lawrence leaned back in Myles' chair and said, "I believe you have an attitude problem, Myles. It's something I'll be sure to take up with the others when I return to Denver."

"And, uh, when will you be doing that?"

Lawrence stood up. "I'm leaving tomorrow night. I'll only need one more day to evaluate the situation here."

Lawrence walked to the door and opened it.

"That leaves you one more day to find both of those men and kill them."

Hammond Myles frowned. He knew whom he would have liked to kill.

Blinky stayed with Canyon and Frank, saying that he didn't know if Nolan would be coming back or not. Canyon left it to Nolan to call, and he agreed that Blinky should stay.

"I intend to come back," Nolan said, "because this is where I live, but who knows what's gonna happen in Denver? Yeah, he can stay."

They had dinner and started talking about how they would get Nolan onto the train. Blinky offered his help, whatever it took.

"We can probably use you, Blinky," Canyon said. "Thanks."

"Aside from getting me on the train," Nolan said, "what are we gonna do when we get to Denver?"

"Well, I think we're really going to have to watch each other's backs, but my plan is to try and get this club to come to me and approach me about joining."

"How are you gonna do that?"

"We know something about the background of the last assassin, and about the man I killed in Washington. They were both in the service, and they were both kicked out. All we have to do is set up that kind of past for me."

"And how do we do that?"

"I've already set it up with Washington, and they'll feed a story to the newspapers. Then we'll make sure that the story ends up in Denver."

"You're taking a big chance," Nolan said.

"That's my job, Frank."

"Well, it's not my job, but I'm doing this to show those people they picked on the wrong guy when they tried to kill me."

"Now the immediate problem is for us to get you on that train without getting you killed," Canyon said.

"A minor problem, right?"

"Maybe," Canyon said as an idea occurred to him, "what we need is some help."

"And where are we supposed to get that from?" Frank Nolan asked.

"How about," Canyon said, "the Dover Hotel?"

"Blinky, did you buy any whiskey, or did Canyon here drink it all up?" Nolan asked. He looked at Canyon and said, "How the hell are we gonna get any help from there? Who'd give it to us? And how are we gonna go there without getting yourself killed? You going there is like me going to the railroad station. Same problem. They're waiting for you—hell, they're probably waiting for both of us."

"Are you finished?"

"I'm not finished," Nolan said, "but I'm out of breath."

"Yes, it's true they're waiting for you," Canyon said, "and they're waiting for me, but they're not waiting for Blinky."

"Me?" Blinky said.

Canyon clapped his hand on the little man's shoulder and said, "Blinky's going to go into the hotel and get us some help."

"How's he gonna do that?" Nolan asked.

"Yeah," Blinky said, "how am I gonna do that?"

"What we need," Canyon said, "is a plan."

"Oh, great," Nolan said, looking at Blinky, "that's just what we need, another plan."

* * *

Blinky was nervous.

He knew that he had offered to do anything he could to help both Canyon O'Grady and Frank Nolan, but he had never done anything like this before, and he wasn't at all sure that he could pull it off, in spite of the assurances he'd received from Canyon and Nolan that they believed he could.

"I'm gonna be scared," he had told them.

"That's good," Nolan had said, exchanging a glance with Canyon. "A scared man is a careful man."

"Right," Canyon said.

"Yeah," Blinky said, "but they're gonna see that I'm scared."

"All the more reason they'll do what you say," Canyon told him. "You can never tell what a scared man will do. They'll do what you say just to keep you from overreacting."

"Right," Frank Nolan agreed.

"I don't know . . ." Blinky said.

"We know, Blinky," Nolan said, putting his hand on the smaller man's shoulder.

"We believe in you," Canyon said, putting his hand on Blinky's other shoulder.

Now Blinky stood outside the Dover Hotel, the weight of the gun heavy in his pocket.

He took a deep breath and went into the hotel.

17

The desk clerk looked up as Blinky entered, and not recognizing him, paid him no mind. In fact, Blinky looked like what he was—a man who made his living driving a cab. As he reached the desk the man behind it didn't even look at him as he spoke.

"Yes? Can I help you?"

Blinky looked around and saw that there was no one else in the lobby. Canyon and Nolan had warned him, though, that there were probably men just a shout away. What he had to do was make sure no one shouted.

"I want to see the manager," Blinky said.

"I'm the assistant manager," Dale Walker said.

"No," Blinky said, "I really need to see the manager."

Now Walker looked up and studied the little man curiously.

"If there is something wrong, I can help you with it," Walker said. "Now what is—"

"I'm afraid I have to insist," Blinky interrupted; repeating the line from memory, "on seeing the manager."

Walker frowned. "You're not a guest of this hotel."

"No," Blinky said, "but it's about a guest."

Walker thought this over a few seconds, then said, "Oh, all right. Wait here."

The man went through a curtained doorway behind him, and Blinky just knew he was going to come back with half a dozen gunmen. When Canyon and Nolan had given him one last chance to pull out, he should have gone back to driving his cab. He could feel the sweat under his arms and in the small of his back and he knew he wasn't cut out for this kind of work. A bead of perspiration fell from his forehead into his eyes and he rubbed at it furiously as the salt stung him.

The assistant manager came through the curtained doorway, and instead of a dozen gunmen he brought with him one other man.

"Are you the manager?" Blinky asked.

"That's right. My name is Mr. Myles. Can I help you with something?"

Myles matched the description Frank Nolan had given Blinky.

"Can we talk over here?" Blinky asked. "Privately?"

He started to back away, and even as Myles started to object he came from around the desk and followed Blinky, who paused far enough from the desk to be out of hearing range.

"I really don't have time for this," Hammond Myles protested. "What is it?"

"Do you know Frank Nolan?" Blinky asked.

He could see the excitement in Myles' eyes at his mention of Frank, though the man only said cautiously, "I don't think I know the name."

"Yeah, you do," Blinky said, putting his hand in his pocket. "You're looking for him and for a redheaded man. I can take you to both of them."

Myles looked at him intently. "In return for what?"

Blinky shrugged. "Money."

"How much money?"

"Not a lot," Blinky said. "I trust you to pay me what the information is worth."

"How do I know you really know where they are?" Myles asked.

"You don't."

Myles reflected briefly, then said, "All right, I'll send a man with you—"

"Nobody else," Blinky interrupted. "It's got to be you, or it's no deal."

"That's silly," Myles said, stammering, "I don't do . . . I don't . . . I have someone who handles these things for me."

"It's got to be you," Blinky repeated.

"I'm sorry," Myles said, "I can't go with you. . . ."

That meant Blinky was going to have to use the gun.

"Mr. Myles," he said, "I guess you can tell I'm really scared here."

"What's that got to do—"

"If I have to take this gun out of my pocket," Blinky said, "it might go off. I'm not very experienced with guns, and I'm so nervous I might pull the trigger by accident."

Myles studied Blinky, trying to decide if he was telling the truth or not. The man certainly looked frightened, Myles thought, but did he have a gun? And would he use it? Myles wondered if he should shout for help, but he was afraid to try.

"I don't believe you would use a gun," Myles finally said weakly, looking down at Blinky's hand in his pocket.

Canyon had told him how to tell if the manager was lying. Watch his eyes, he had said. If he can't look you in the eyes, then he's lying. Blinky looked the man in the eyes, and Myles looked away uncomfortably. Blinky said what Canyon O'Grady had told him to say in this situation.

"To tell you the God's honest truth, mister," he said, "I don't know if I would either. Should we find out?"

Myles bit his bottom lip while he contemplated the situation, and then said, "What do you want me to do?"

"Walk outside and get into my cab."

"What do I tell my assistant?"

"Nothing," Blinky said. "You're the boss, ain't you? Just walk outside and get into my cab. Let's go."

They started for the door, Myles walking ahead of Blinky. Dale Walker looked up from the desk and saw them leaving.

"Mr. Myles!" he called.

Myles stopped walking and Blinky said, "Keep going," and the man started forward again.

"Mr. Myles," Walker called again, and when the manager didn't answer, Walker just figured that he was being ignored again.

If he was lucky, maybe the little man would kidnap Myles and not bring him back.

No, he couldn't get that lucky.

Outside the hotel, Hammond Myles climbed into the cab and Blinky climbed atop it and drove away.

Inside the hotel, Talbot Lawrence came down from his room and asked Dale Walker, "Is Myles in his office?"

"No, sir."

Lawrence waited, and when the other man didn't elaborate he wondered if everyone in Chicago was an idiot. He was going to have to recommend to the board that they find another stopover point.

"Where is he, then?"

"I don't know," Walker said. "He just left with someone and didn't tell me where he was going."

"You mean he just walked out? Does it have something to do with Frank Nolan?"

"I don't know, Mr. Lawrence," Walker said.

"Well, it's irresponsible for him just to walk out without a word."

"I called out to him, but he ignored me."

Lawrence thought about it, and decided that it didn't sound like something Hammond Myles would do. The man was an idiot, but he liked running the hotel. He wouldn't just walk away from it.

"Did he leave with anyone?"

"Some little man who came in and said he had to see the manager."

"Did Myles leave willingly?"

"I guess so."

"What do you mean, you guess so? Did he or didn't he?" Lawrence asked impatiently.

"As far as I could tell," Walker said, wary now because Lawrence was becoming annoyed, and Lawrence was a powerful man. In fact, Walker reflected, Mr. Lawrence had the power to fire Myles as manager and name a replacement.

"I can have someone go out and look for him," Walker offered.

"Do that," Lawrence said. "I'll be in his office. Call me when you find him."

"Yes, sir," Walker said. "I'll take care of it."

Lawrence went behind the desk and through the curtained doorway. He couldn't wait to get back to Denver.

Blinky drove around for a while to make sure he wasn't followed and then headed for the deserted livery stable. He ignored Hammond Myles' attempts to talk to him, and he drove very fast—fast to discourage any thoughts his passenger might have of leaping from the cab. Not that he thought Myles would really try anything like that. Much to Blinky's amazement, it was clear that Myles was more afraid of guns and violence than he himself was. The man was a coward. Otherwise the plan would never have worked.

When they arrived, it was Canyon O'Grady who came out to meet them. Nolan stayed inside.

Blinky dropped down from his perch and said to Canyon, "I ain't never doing something like this again."

"You did fine, Blinky."

"I still ain't never doing it again."

"Who do we have here, Blinky?"

"This is Mr. Myles, the manager of the Dover Hotel. You can get out now, Mr. Myles."

Myles climbed out of the back of the cab and stood in front of Canyon, trying for all he was worth to maintain his dignity.

"And who are you, sir?" Myles asked.

Canyon took off his hat, revealing his red hair.

"My name is O'Grady, Mr. Myles."

Myles frowned and said, "Are you the man with the key?"

"That's me," Canyon said, "and if we can go inside I'll introduce you to a man you've been looking for."

Myles froze. "Frank Nolan?"

"That's right," Canyon said. "Frank Nolan."

"But . . . he'll kill me!"

"Why would he want to do that?" Canyon asked. "Just because you tried to have *him* killed?"

"That wasn't my idea!"

"Well," Canyon said, "come on, you can explain that to Frank Nolan. He's a very understanding man."

Canyon and Blinky walked Hammond Myles into the livery, where Frank Nolan was waiting.

"This is him, huh?" Nolan said, playing the role Canyon had set up for him. "This is the son of a bitch that tried to have me killed."

He took a menacing step toward Myles, who tried to hide behind Canyon.

"Keep him away from me!" the man said. "It wasn't my fault!"

"You're in charge, aren't you?" Canyon asked. "You give the orders."

"I give the orders here in Chicago," Myles said, "but I'm not the boss."

"Who is?" Canyon asked.

Myles hesitated.

"Let's stop talking to him and kill him," Nolan said. "It's him we have right here and now."

"No!" Myles cried. "The boss's name is Lawrence, Talbot Lawrence. He's here in Chicago now."

"He's the one sending out all of the assassins?" Canyon asked, turning to face Myles.

"You know about that?" the hotel manager asked in dismayed surprise.

"We know quite a lot, Mr. Myles," Canyon said, "but we need to know more."

"Lawrence is at the hotel," Myles said. "You could go and get him now."

"We don't want him now," Canyon said. "Where does Lawrence work out of?"

"Denver," Myles said. "He has an office in Denver that he uses as a front."

"What kind of office?"

"He's an attorney."

"An attorney?" Canyon said. "Really? That's interesting. Does he practice in Denver?"

"Denver and Washington," Hammond Myles said.

Washington. Somehow that didn't surprise Canyon.

"And he's in charge of the whole operation?" he asked. "He runs the show?"

"No," Myles said, "he's just one of the men involved. There's something he calls the board that makes all the decisions."

"How democratic," Canyon said. "And when is he going back to Denver?"

"Tomorrow night."

Canyon looked at Nolan. They'd be in Denver a full day before Lawrence. Would that be enough time to put their plan into effect? Probably not. Once they left Chicago, Lawrence would most likely figure out where they had gone. If they had the time they could get to him now, but Canyon wasn't sure that was the right thing to do. If they junked their first plan, they could wait for Lawrence to arrive in Denver and then follow him. Canyon decided that their best bet now was to get on the train to Denver, because that was where the assassins were originating. During the train ride they could work out a new plan.

"Don't let him kill me," Myles said, pleading and cowering behind Canyon.

Canyon realized that while he had been ruminating, Frank Nolan had taken a few more steps toward Myles, and he signaled Nolan to back off.

"All right, Mr. Myles," Canyon said. "Now we're going to sit down and relax and talk like civilized men, and you're going to tell us all you know about this organization."

"The killers' club," Myles said helpfully. "That's what they call themselves."

"That's fine," Canyon said. "Let's go and sit down and talk all about it."

18

Hammond Myles told them all he knew about the killers' club. Apparently it was run by a group of men with extremist political positions diametrically opposed to those of American democracy. This group saw the furor over slavery in America as a weapon to attain its own ends. Its aim was to eliminate leaders or potential leaders of both parties, in government or out, leaving a weakened nation unable to function. Assassination was their tool.

"So they train—or condition—assassins and will send them out to do political assassinations," Canyon said.

"Yes," Myles said, "but you sound like you knew that already."

"Not the particulars," Canyon said. "We know of about half a dozen assassinations they've carried out over the past few months."

"Half a dozen?" Myles said, snorting derisively. "There have been close to twenty."

"Twenty?" Canyon said. "As far as I know, Senator Brown is the only politician there has been an attempt on."

"Test cases," Myles said. "Most of the others were test cases too. But some of those people—a rancher in Kentucky, a banker in Minnesota—had political opinions and ambitions. They had to be taken care of before they got into power."

"I see," Canyon said. "Get rid of the people already in power and the people who might replace them."

"What are you left with?" Nolan said.

"They'd be left with their own people," Canyon said,

looking at Nolan, "and before long, they'd have puppet politicians in power."

"Jesus," Nolan said, wide-eyed, "they're trying to take over the country!"

"And it's up to us to stop them," Canyon said grimly.

Nolan stood up. "We'd better tie Myles up and get going."

"No," Canyon said, "he's coming with us."

"To Denver?" Nolan asked.

"No," Canyon said, "just to the station." He looked at Blinky. "We need your cab."

"Sure, I'll take you—"

"No," Canyon said, "you're not coming to the station. I've got something else for you to do."

"What?"

"I'll explain," Canyon said, putting his arm around the driver's shoulders. "Come on, let's get ready to go."

On the way out Canyon explained to Blinky what he wanted him to do. It was much easier than what he had just done.

"We'll take you part of the way," Canyon said, "but then we have to get to the station fast because we don't want to miss this train."

"I understand."

"Can you handle it?"

"After what I did today?" Blinky said. "Sure, I can handle it."

"Good."

They stepped outside to check the area, and then Nolan came out with Hammond Myles. They all got into the cab and Canyon got up top to drive.

"You be gentle with Mirabelle," Blinky called up to him. "She's a little old and don't take kindly to the feel of the whip."

"I'll be careful," Canyon called back down. He picked up the reins and said to Mirabelle, "Come on, girl, let's show this man you aren't as old as he thinks you are."

He left the whip alone, but he slapped the horse with the

reins, and she responded as if she understood what he had said.

"Easy," Blinky shouted as they started off down the street at a gallop.

Canyon stopped the cab at the same location he and Blinky had left it at earlier.

"Out," he said to Hammond Myles.

"I hope Blinky gets his part done in time," Nolan said, getting out after Myles.

"What are you going to do with me?" Myles asked fearfully.

"It's not what we're going to do with you, Mr. Myles," Canyon said, "it's what you're going to do with us."

"What's he gonna do with us?" Nolan asked.

"He's going to walk us onto the train," Canyon said, "and hopefully we can do it without a shot being fired."

"B-but . . . I could get killed if there's shooting!" Myles said, almost blubbering.

"Then you'd better make sure there isn't any shooting," Canyon said. "These are your men and you better make sure the four of them think we're just a couple more of your men who you're putting on the train."

"Six."

"What?"

"There are six men at the station," Myles said. "Mr. Lawrence made me add two more."

"That's great," Nolan said. "Six against two. If shooting does start, we're outgunned three to one."

"We've still got our ace in the hole."

"Him?" Nolan asked, pointing to Myles. "I'd feel better with a pair of deuces."

"No, not him," Canyon said. "I'm talking about Blinky."

"Oh."

"Look, Frank," Canyon said, "if you don't want to do this—" He broke off and looked at Myles. "Mr. Myles, we're going to walk just a few feet away. If you move, I'll shoot you in the knee. Understand?''

"I—I understand.''

"Come on,'' Canyon said, taking Nolan's arm and walking him out of earshot.

"Frank, like you've said already,'' he told him in a low voice, "this isn't your job.''

"No, no, no,'' Nolan said. "I still want to take these people down. I mean, who wants a bunch of murderers running the country, right?''

"Right.''

"It's just that . . .'' Nolan leaned closer to Canyon and said a trifle wistfully, "If I had known what I was up against, what was at stake, I just wonder how much I could have turned it into.'' He rubbed his index and middle fingers together with his thumb, wondering.

"Frank,'' Canyon said, "I *can* trust you on this, can't I? I mean, you're not getting any ideas, are you?''

"Canyon,'' Nolan said, dropping his hand to his side, "would I turn on you?''

Canyon remembered abruptly that Frank Nolan was a man who usually thought of himself first. He wasn't helping Canyon because he wanted to save the country, he just wanted to get back at the people who'd tried to kill him. What would he do if he thought he could walk away from this with a lot of money in his pocket?

"I hope not, Frank,'' Canyon said. "Don't forget, these people tried to kill you once already.''

"How could I forget?''

Canyon looked over at Myles, who was standing rooted to the spot where they'd left him.

"All right, then,'' Canyon said, "let's get this under way. We've got about twenty minutes to make that train.''

Nolan looked around and said, "Where's Blinky when you need him?''

* * *

Talbot Lawrence came out of Myles' office and collared Dale Walker.

"Have you located Myles yet?"

"Well, no, sir," Walker said nervously. "I've had men out looking, but we can't find him. Don't worry, though, I'll take care of it—"

"That's been my problem," Lawrence said, "I've been letting incompetents take care of everything. Get me four men. I'll be taking them with me to the railroad station. Something's wrong here, and that's where I think it's all going to be sorted out."

"I'll come too—"

"No!" Lawrence said. "Do me a favor and don't. Just get me those men!"

They walked up to the station with Hammond Myles between them. He had been told that if he tried anything, he'd be killed immediately.

"At that point, Mr. Myles," Canyon said, speaking very slowly, "we'd have nothing to lose. Understand?"

Myles nodded, his mouth too dry to speak.

In order to get to the platform to board the train they had to walk through a large wooden station building. As they walked in, Canyon saw four men stationed at different points. The other two men must be on the platform, he decided. The men straightened up when they saw Hammond Myles with Nolan and Canyon and began to exchange glances, obviously wondering what they were supposed to do.

"Is one of these men in charge of the others?" Canyon asked.

"Yes," Myles said, inclining his head toward one of the four watchers, "that one."

"What's his name?"

"Sawyer."

"Get him over here," Canyon said. "Just tell him that you're sending two men to Denver."

"He'll want to know why."

"No, he won't," Canyon said. "You're the boss, aren't you?"

"Yes, that's right," Myles said, as if talking to himself. "I'm the boss."

He waved his hand at Sawyer, who pushed away from the wall he was leaning against and walked over.

"What's going on, boss?" Sawyer asked. "Isn't one of these men the fella we've been waiting for?"

"I'm sending these two men to Denver," Myles said. "We've worked out our disagreements."

Sawyer waited, but when Myles didn't explain further he just shrugged and said, "Okay. How much longer do we have to stay here?"

"Until I tell you to leave," Myles said, and the man backed off with his hands raised. "Hey, you're the boss."

"Go back to your position."

Sawyer turned and walked back to his wall.

"Come on," Canyon said, "let's get on that train. It's almost time."

They walked through the station building to the other end, where a wide doorway would lead them to the platform. They had almost reached it when Canyon heard something behind them, some commotion.

"Stop them!" someone shouted. "Stop those men! Kill them!"

Canyon, Nolan, and Myles all turned.

"Who's that?" Canyon asked.

"That's Lawrence—" was all Myles had time to say before a bullet slammed into his chest. He slid to the floor between them and Canyon knew there was nothing that could be done for him.

"Jesus," Nolan said, drawing his gun.

Canyon turned around in time to see the two men from the platform coming through the door. They still didn't know exactly what was going on and hadn't yet drawn their guns. Canyon shot them before they could join the fray.

That left the four men who had been waiting for them plus Lawrence and the two men he had brought with him.

Nolan was down on one knee, returning fire selectively. Firing hastily would just use up precious bullets, and in this kind of situation reloading was not an option. They had to get on that train.

Canyon saw a man spin and go down, and then turned to his right and fired. Sawyer clutched his belly and doubled over. Nearby Canyon heard the train begin moving out. The engineer probably couldn't hear the shooting over the sound of the locomotive.

"Let's go, Frank," Canyon said, grabbing Nolan's shoulder.

Bullets chewed up the walls on either side of them and then the floor in front of them as they backed through the doorway onto the platform. It had been a lucky break that Canyon had been able to take care of the two men from the platform, or he and Nolan would now be caught in a deadly crossfire.

Canyon couldn't see Lawrence and figured the man had probably run for cover. The four remaining men were advancing on them, spread out across the station, firing as they came.

"Get on the train!" Canyon shouted. "I'll hold them."

Nolan was going to argue, but thought better of it.

"Here," he said, handing Canyon his gun and then jumping for the slowly moving train. There might have been two or three shots left in each weapon, and then Canyon would have to run for the train himself.

That was when the front doors of the station opened and policemen poured in. Their four adversaries turned to face the police.

"Thanks, Blinky," Canyon said half aloud, and turned and ran for the train. Nolan was already aboard, and the engine was picking up speed. Canyon holstered his gun and stuck Nolan's into his belt. He couldn't hear if there was shooting behind him because the noise of the locomotive was so loud. He ran alongside the cars until he reached Nolan, who had his hands outstretched. Canyon reached out and their hands locked. Nolan hauled him up to the car, and they were on their way to Denver.

They found their way to their private car and Canyon handed Nolan's gun back to him. Before they even spoke— and while they caught their breath—they sat down and reloaded their weapons and holstered them.

"Myles is dead," Canyon said.

"Did you see Blinky?" Nolan asked.

"No," Canyon said. "I'm sure he's all right."

"He's going to have to explain all of this to the police, since he's the one who got them there," Nolan said. "They might hold him."

"He might be safer if they do," Canyon said. "When we get to Denver I'll send a telegram to Washington and have them send one to the Chicago police."

"What about this Mr. Lawrence?" Nolan asked. "Did you see what happened to him?"

"He disappeared when the shooting started."

"He'll be sending a telegram of his own to Denver," Nolan said. "They're gonna be waiting for us when we get off the train. There goes your plan about going into their organization as a potential assassin. What do we do now?"

"I don't know," Canyon said, "but we've got a long ride ahead of us to try and figure it out."

"Oh, good," Nolan said, staring out the window, "we get to come up with another plan."

"If we keep at it," Canyon said, "we're bound to come up with one that works."

19

During the ride to Denver they bounced plans off one another. What it came down to was this: they were going to have to check out Lawrence's offices and Lawrence himself. They'd have a full day before Lawrence arrived. When he did, they wanted to be there at the station so they could follow him.

"Unless we find something out that first day, we're just going to have to wait and see if he leads us anywhere," Canyon said.

"That could take a long time," Nolan commented. "A lot of other people could die while we're waiting."

"I don't think so," Canyon said. "I don't think the club will try anything more until they've dealt with us."

"Tried," Nolan said. "At least say until they've 'tried' to deal with us. You make it sound like there's nothing we can do to stop it."

"If I felt that way," Canyon said, "I wouldn't be on this train."

"And that's something else we're gonna have to deal with," Nolan said.

"What is it?"

"How are we gonna get off this train in Denver?" Nolan asked. "You know there are gonna be men there waiting for us, and I don't think we're gonna be as lucky as we were in Chicago."

"Oh, that," Canyon said. "I've already got that figured out."

"You do?"

"Yes," Canyon said, "I have a plan."

"I can't wait."

"We're not getting off the train in Denver," Canyon said, "we're going to get off outside of Denver."

"And how are we going to get the train to stop just to let us off?" Nolan asked. "Put a gun to the engineer's head?"

"We don't have to get the train to stop."

"Oh, sure," Nolan said, "we're gonna get off the train while it's moving, right?"

Canyon didn't answer. He turned his head to look out the window. He could see Nolan's reflection, and the man looked aghast as he realized that he was right.

"We're gonna get off the train while it's still *moving*?" he repeated.

"It shouldn't be too hard," Canyon said. "There's got to be a twist or a turn somewhere where the train will slow down. All we have to do is be ready and jump off."

"And land without breaking an arm or a leg . . . or our necks."

"Don't be such a pessimist, Frank," Canyon said. "Just think about the number of guns that will be waiting for us in Denver, and what's the alternative?"

Nolan thought for a few moments, a helpless look on his face.

"We've still got some time," Canyon said. "Come up with another plan and I'll be all for it."

"You're a son of a bitch, you know that? I didn't know, when you got me involved in this, that I was going to be jumping from a moving train."

"I got you involved?" Canyon said. "Correct me if I'm wrong, but these people tried to kill you even before I got to Chicago."

"Yeah, yeah, you're right," Nolan acknowledged sourly.

"It'll be fine, Frank," Canyon said, slapping the man on the knee. "Look, I'll even jump off the train first, huh? If

I get killed, you can take your chances in the railroad station.''

Nolan stared at Canyon, evidently trying to think of a good comeback, and then finally settled for repeating, ''You're a son of a bitch, you know that?''

''Let's get some sleep,'' Canyon said. ''We'll be nearing Denver tomorrow morning, and we want to be awake when we jump.''

After a few minutes of silence Nolan's voice woke Canyon just as he was dozing off.

''And after we jump, how far are we gonna have to *walk?*''

The next morning they found a conductor and questioned him as to how far they now were from Denver. Using that information, they were going to try to work out the best time and place to jump from the train. When they figured that they were about half an hour from Denver they positioned themselves outside one of the passenger cars, waiting for an opportunity to jump.

''We're gonna break our necks,'' Nolan said.

''Stop worrying, Frank,'' Canyon said. ''Even if we wait until the train slows down to pull into the station, we should still be able to avoid the men who are waiting for us. We just have to make sure we avoid getting off the train in the station.''

Nolan muttered something Canyon didn't hear.

''What did you say?''

''I said some plan.''

Canyon didn't comment, and they continued to wait for the best time to jump.

Suddenly, Denver sprang up in front of them.

''Hey, I can see Denver,'' Nolan said.

''Time to get off,'' Canyon answered.

''We're not slowing down.''

''Yes, we are,'' Canyon said. ''Look.''

Sure enough, the train was starting to slow down as it

entered the city limits. Ahead, they could see that the front of the train was rounding a curve.

"We have to go now, before we come into view from the station," Canyon urged.

"Maybe we should just shoot it out—" Nolan started, but he was cut off as Canyon pushed him from behind and said, "Jump!"

Canyon launched himself after Nolan and landed, rolling, to minimize the impact. When he stopped rolling he looked around for Nolan and saw him staggering toward him.

"Did you break anything?" Canyon asked.

"Not yet," Nolan said, and swung at Canyon, who ducked beneath the blow and grabbed Nolan from behind.

"Take it easy, Frank," Canyon said. "We've got enough trouble without fighting between ourselves."

"Okay, okay," Nolan said, "let me go."

Canyon released the man and stepped away from him. Nolan took a deep breath to calm himself and then began brushing himself off.

"What do we do now?" he asked. "We have no fresh clothes or anything."

"We'll buy some," Canyon said. "Right now, let's walk into Denver and try to locate Lawrence's office."

Still brushing themselves off, they started walking, Frank Nolan rubbing his ass, because that's what he had landed on.

When they entered the city limits they quickly ascertained where they were by looking at street signs, and then asked someone for directions to High Street. On the way to the Chicago railroad station Canyon had asked Hammond Myles where Talbot Lawrence's office was located, and he had said it was on High Street, but he didn't know the exact address.

They found High Street and did the only thing they could. They started walking, looking at all the windows and doors for names.

"If he's an attorney," Canyon said, "there should be a

sign by the doors or stenciled on the window. You walk on that side of the street, and I'll walk on this side.''

"Right."

Along the way Canyon picked up a copy of the *Denver Dispatch* and leafed through it until he found what he was looking for. General Wheeler had come through. There was a story about a "Captain Canyon O'Grady," who had been drummed out of the army for excessive violence. It went on to give the opinion that O'Grady was "murderous."

It was the perfect story for an organization like this killers' club, if they were looking for recruits. The problem was that Talbot Lawrence had probably already telegraphed Canyon's description to his people in Denver. Of course, Lawrence didn't know Canyon's name, and the description of a tall, red-haired man would fit a number of people. Lawrence wasn't due in Denver until tomorrow, so the plan could still work if they could put it into effect today. That seemed to be asking a lot, however. Meanwhile, as far as the world at large was concerned, Canyon O'Grady was a disgraced, homicidal ex-army officer. The news article gave Denver as his home, saying that he was returning there in disgrace, and even gave an address. That would spare them having to find a hotel.

Canyon looked up from his reading to see Nolan coming across the street toward him.

"I found it," Nolan said. "What're you doing reading the newspaper?"

Canyon showed him the story and waited until he'd read it.

"This is wonderful," Nolan said. "You're branded a lunatic, and we may not even be able to use the plan."

"We'll see about that," Canyon said. "Meanwhile, show me Lawrence's office."

Across the street, in the offices of Talbot Lawrence, Attorney-at-Law, Andrew Huston walked into Samuel Dean's office while Dean was intently reading the newspaper.

"What's so interesting?" Huston asked.

Dean looked up. "We may have found another recruit."

Huston and Dean, along with Lawrence, made up the Board of Directors of what they called the killers' club. In effect they were partners, although the law office bore Lawrence's name alone. As far as the law office was concerned Lawrence was titled the senior partner, but in the club they were all supposedly equal.

Huston and Dean, like Lawrence, were in their fifties, and shared the same political ambitions and lust for power.

"Where?" Huston asked.

Dean turned the newspaper around so that Huston could see it. The other man read the news item quickly and said, "He sounds like a likely candidate, all right, but the telegram from Talbot warned us against doing any recruiting until he gets back."

"Talbot thinks his word is law," Dean said. "We should show him that he's wrong."

"That's all well and good," Huston said, "but how do you intend to find this—O'Grady, is it?"

"It says right at the end of the article that he's gone home in disgrace."

"And where is home?" Huston asked, frowning down at the newspaper. He'd obviously missed that part when he'd skimmed the article.

Dean reached across the desk and pointed to that part of the news item, saying, "Denver."

Canyon and Nolan crossed the street, and Nolan pointed out the large window that said *Talbot Lawrence & Associates. Attorneys-at-Law.*

"What do we do now?" Nolan asked. "Go up there and ask them if they're sending out assassins?"

Canyon still had the newspaper in his hand. He shook it and said, "This could still work."

"How?"

"Since the story appeared today, we can assume that they've read it today."

"Who's they?"

"Myles told us there was a board of directors," Canyon said. "Lawrence is in Denver, so the other members of the board must be looking for recruits."

"So what are you suggesting?"

"We've got a full day before Lawrence gets here," Canyon said. "Let's go to my address, as it appears here in the paper, and wait and see what happens. If nothing happens we can always catch Lawrence when he arrives tomorrow and follow him.

Nolan thought it over and then started shaking his head. "There's another thing to take into consideration here, Canyon."

"What's that?"

"If you go to that address and wait, nobody is going to have to go looking for you," Nolan said. "They'll know right where you are. That's going to make you a mighty easy target."

"So what's your suggestion?"

"I think you should go to the address, but I think I should stay outside and watch your back," Nolan said. "After all, I think that's why you brought me along on this, isn't it?"

"My God, Frank," Canyon said, "I think you've come up with a plan."

20

The address given in the newspaper as Kill-crazy Canyon O'Grady's home was a rundown section of Denver that much resembled the area in Chicago where Frank Nolan lived.

"Hey, I feel right at home," Nolan said, with a big smile. "Look, there's a saloon across the street just like the White Horse. That's where I'll be."

"Try to stay sober, huh?" Canyon said.

"I don't have a drinking problem, O'Grady," Nolan said, and then added, "at least, not when I'm working."

"Glad to hear it."

"How are you going to get into your new home?" Nolan asked.

"I guess I'll knock on the door," Canyon said, "and see what happens."

"I think we're going to be doing a lot of that today," Nolan said. "Waiting to see what happens."

"Let's just both stay awake and alert while we're doing it."

"Don't worry, Canyon," Nolan said. "I'll be watching your back."

"Just watch my back and not some saloon girl's front."

"I'll see you later, partner," Nolan said, and crossed the street.

Canyon watched him until he entered the saloon, then turned and walked to the front door of his new address. He knocked on the door and was surprised when the door was opened by a beautiful woman with long dark hair and a full figure. She appeared to be in her late thirties, and he suspected that by the time she was forty-five she would be fat. Right now she was best described as voluptuous.

"Can I help you?"

"My name is O'Grady."

She looked him up and down for a few moments, then said, "Wait here." She disappeared inside for about ten seconds and then reappeared.

"Here's your key," she said. "Your room is upstairs."

"Uh, thank you."

"I'm the landlady," she said. "My name is Mrs. Grimsley —and before you ask, there is no Mr. Grimsley. Not anymore."

Canyon wasn't sure what he was supposed to say in response to that, so he didn't say anything at all. Instead, he asked a question.

"Which is my room?"

"Right at the head of these stairs," she said, indicating the stairway behind her.

He had to squeeze by her to get in, and her full breasts pushed against his chest.

He started up the stairs, then turned and said, "I'm expecting some visitors tonight."

"Men or women?"

"Men."

She waved her hand and said, "I'll send them right up."

"Thank you."

As he went up the stairs he could sense her eyes on him the whole time. He could still feel her firm breasts against his chest. Another time, another place, he thought. . . .

The room was bare but for a bed and a chest of drawers, neither of which he would get much use out of. He did sit on the bed, but he didn't lie down. He kept his holster on, and sat quietly in the room so that he could hear everything. He wanted to be ready just in case someone came who wasn't there to talk.

* * *

Across the street Frank Nolan got himself a beer and sat by the window, so he could clearly see the front of the building Canyon had entered. If anything happened in the back, Canyon O'Grady was going to have to be alert enough to take care of it.

Two of the girls working in the place came over to him, but he rejected their offers. He hated to do it, because they were both pretty in a slutty sort of way, not like the girls in the White Horse, who were nice girls. These girls were really more his type, and if he wasn't working, he probably would have taken both of them upstairs, where they said they had rooms.

O'Grady, he thought, the things I do for you.

Nolan got halfway through his second beer before he saw some movement across the street. A carriage pulled up and two men got out. They were well dressed, and didn't look anything like Nolan's idea of assassins.

Nolan forgot about the beer and concentrated on looking out the window.

True to her word, when the two men knocked on the door and asked for Canyon O'Grady, Mrs. Grimsley sent them right up.

Canyon heard the footsteps on the stairs before the knock came at the door. He doubted they'd announce themselves to the landlady, then knock on the door and kill him, so he left his gun in his holster as he opened the door.

"Mr. O'Grady?" He could only see the man who was speaking. The stairway was not wide enough for the two of them to stand shoulder to shoulder, and the second man was hidden behind the first. This man was in his forties, had a well-fed look, and was dressed expensively.

"That's me."

"May we come in?"

"That depends on who you are and what you want."

"What we want," the man said, "is to make you a rich man. Who we are we can tell you when you let us in."

Canyon waited a few moments, then stepped back from the door to admit them. The second man closed the door behind him.

"All right," Canyon said, "you're in. Who are you?"

The spokesman said, "This is Mr. Jones and I am Mr. Smith."

"And I'm Mr. Brown. Is this a joke?"

Mr. "Smith" reached into his pocket and took out a thousand-dollar bill. He handed it to Canyon.

"Does that look like a joke, Mr. O'Grady?"

"It looks like a thousand dollars," Canyon said, hoping he sounded impressed. "Is there more where this came from?"

Mr. Smith smiled. "Much more."

"Who do I have to kill?" Canyon asked, and even as he said it he knew it was too cute.

"Whoever we say," Mr. Smith said.

Canyon paused a beat and then said, "You're kidding."

"Were you kidding?"

Canyon looked down at the thousand-dollar bill and said, "For a few more of these, I guess I'd kill somebody. I mean, what else have I got going for me?"

"We need men, Mr. O'Grady," Smith said, "good men."

"Good at what?"

"What have we been talking about?" Smith said. "Good at killing. Are you good at killing, Mr. O'Grady?"

"Sure," Canyon said, "I was a soldier. I'm very good at killing, but . . . is this all for real?"

"We're being very candid, Mr. O'Grady," Smith said. "We read about you in the newspaper today, and you sounded like the kind of man we've been looking for."

"What do I have to do?" Canyon asked. "Just kill who you tell me to?"

"Not quite," Smith said. "You'll have to agree to undergo some training first."

"Where does this training take place?"

"Have you ever been to Arizona?"

"Once or twice," Canyon said, then looked down at the thousand-dollar bill he was holding and said, "but for a few more of these I'd go again."

"Be ready to leave in the morning," Smith said.

"So soon?"

"Is that a problem?"

"No, of course not."

"We will send someone for you."

"How will I know who it is?"

Smith smiled and tapped the bill in Canyon's hand.

"He will have another one of these for you. Will that identify him sufficiently?"

"It'll do."

The other man had never spoken. He was taller than his colleague, but about the same age. Now he opened the door so they could leave.

"Where will you be tomorrow?" Canyon asked them.

"Don't worry, Mr. O'Grady," Smith said, "you'll be seeing us tomorrow."

"I'll be looking forward to it."

Smith and Jones both nodded—Jones' first indication that he could even hear what was going on—and went back down the stairs. Canyon closed the door and listened intently until he heard the downstairs door close. Then he opened the door again and ran downstairs.

When he got to the front door he opened it a crack to look out, and he saw the two men climb into a carriage. As they pulled away he opened the door and frantically waved at the saloon across the street.

Frank Nolan saw the two men leave, and moments later Canyon O'Grady was in the doorway, waving his arms. Nolan got up, left the saloon, and ran across the street.

"I don't believe it," Canyon said.

"What?"

"They recruited me already."

"What?"

"We have to follow them," Canyon said, pulling the door closed behind him.

"How?"

"Come on," Canyon said, starting off on the run.

"We can't follow them on foot!" Nolan called out.

"Maybe we'll find a cab along the way," Canyon called back. "Come on, Frank!"

They ran, but they didn't find a cab in that part of town and finally had to stop.

"We lost them, damn it!" Canyon swore.

Breathing hard, Frank Nolan said, "Look . . . let's go back to that saloon . . . and you can tell me what happened."

"They want me to go to Arizona in the morning, Frank," Canyon said. "That's where they do their training."

"That means the train again."

"Probably," Canyon said. "There are other ways, but that would be the quickest. We're just going to have to wait until they send someone to pick me up in the morning."

"Lawrence will be getting here in the morning," Nolan said.

"Well, hopefully he won't get in at the same time I'm going out."

"What if he gets in before you leave?"

"We'll have to deal with that when the time comes."

"And what am I supposed to do while you get on a train to Arizona."

"Buy a ticket."

"With what?" Nolan asked.

"Here." Canyon took out the thousand-dollar bill and handed it to him. "Use that."

"Where did you get this?" Nolan asked, after he'd retrieved his fallen jaw.

"From them," Canyon said. "They called themselves Smith and Jones, although Smith did all the talking. He gave me the bill and said there were a lot more where that came from."

"Jesus," Nolan said, staring at the bill, fingering it

carefully as if to make sure it was real. "Canyon, maybe we should reconsider our position—"

"Are you going to kill people for a thousand dollars, Frank?"

"Well," Nolan said, "not for *one* thousand—"

"And remember," Canyon said, "they don't pay off their assassins. A hundred of those wouldn't be any good to you if you're dead."

"Okay, okay," Nolan said, "you've got a point. Let's go back to the saloon, huh? We can break this up on a couple of dozen beers." Nolan folded the thousand-dollar bill and tucked it into his pocket.

"I've got to find a telegraph office," Canyon said. "I have to tell Washington about Arizona. They've got to have a company of cavalrymen waiting to move when we give the signal. Who knows how many men they have at this training site."

"Even if we find an office it'll probably be closed," Nolan argued.

"Then we'll just have to open it," Canyon said. "Come on, Frank."

"Okay," Nolan said, "but this time can we just *walk*?"

21

The next morning Canyon was waiting for his ride. Across the street Nolan was waiting in the doorway of the saloon, which was closed. Once again they were going to have to take the chance that Nolan would be able to find a cab and follow behind Canyon. Maybe it would be easier to find one in the daylight. If not, they decided that Nolan—when he did find transportation—would have to go directly to the train station.

Before returning to the saloon the night before they had managed to find a telegraph office and, although it was closed, they did not let that stop them. They broke in, and Canyon sent his message to Washington. It was a long one, giving details about Chicago, Denver, and Arizona.

They had returned to the saloon, had a couple of beers, and then gone up to Canyon's room, where they took turns keeping watch and sleeping on the bed. Before first light Nolan left the room, just in case Canyon's escort arrived extra early.

All they knew about Lawrence's arrival was that if he took the train at the same time they had, he'd be arriving about 10 A.M. If Canyon's escort came at or about 8 A.M., then it was a pretty safe bet they'd miss Lawrence. What happened then was anyone's guess. Lawrence had never seen Canyon, so when the lawyer's partners told him about the man they had recruited and sent on to Arizona, maybe he wouldn't react.

And maybe he would, and when Canyon got off the train

in Arizona there'd be a huge reception waiting for him—
with a pine box.

That was a chance he was going to have to take.

About 8:20 A.M. a carriage pulled up in front of the
building and two men got out. They knocked on the
downstairs door and Canyon answered it, by previous
arrangement with Mrs. Grimsley. Canyon didn't know what
her connection was with anything, but he didn't want to get
her involved any more than was necessary. She had asked
too few questions to be just an innocent bystander, and his
best guess would be that she worked for General Wheeler,
probably as an agent in place for him in Denver.

"Gentlemen," Canyon said to the two men, who did not
at all resemble Smith and Jones of the night before. They
were dressed well—though not as expensively as Smith and
Jones—but they were still hired toughs.

"Are you O'Grady?" one of them said.

"That's me."

"Let's go."

"Don't you have something for me?"

A glance passed between the two men, and it was obvious
that they had been hoping he wouldn't ask. Grudgingly, the
spokesman of the two reached into his pocket and came out
with a thousand-dollar bill.

"All right," Canyon said, taking it, "now let's go."

"You got any bags?" the other man asked.

"I travel light."

He followed them to the carriage and got in the back with
one of them while the other drove. As they pulled away, he
fervently hoped that Frank would be close on their trail.

At 8:30 A.M. a train pulled into the Denver railroad station
from Chicago, and Talbot Lawrence got off. He was met
by Dean.

"Welcome back, Talbot," Dean said, taking his partner's
bag from him. "I have a carriage waiting out front."

"How is everything at this end?" Lawrence asked.

"Running smoothly."

"And any word from Arizona?"

"Also running smoothly."

"I wish I could say the same for things back east," Lawrence said. "We are going to have to make new arrangements in Washington and Chicago."

"That's too bad," Dean said, as they reached the carriage outside the station. "It'll hold up our timetable."

"Not by much," Lawrence said. "What about the men I telegraphed you about. Have they appeared?"

"No sign of them," Dean said.

"They didn't get off a train yesterday?" Lawrence asked. "Did you have men at the station?"

"We did have men here," Dean said, "but they didn't get off."

"Well, they must have gotten off the train before it pulled in. They're here," Lawrence said. "I *know* they're here, and they're going to have to be taken care of."

"We'll take care of them, Talbot, don't worry," Dean said. Dean put Lawrence's bag in the back of the carriage as Lawrence climbed in. Dean climbed in next to him and signaled the driver to go.

"I'll want extra men at the office, in case they come there," Lawrence said.

"Why would they show up there?" Dean asked. "How would they even know about it?"

"That fool Myles had to have told them."

"Did he say he did?"

"He's dead," Lawrence said. "He was killed in a gun fight at the station which I barely escaped. The police arrived and killed all of our men, and those two—Nolan and his partner—got away on the train."

"You don't know the partner's name?"

"No," Lawrence said, "all I know is that he's a big red-haired man."

Dean stared at his partner. "Big and red-haired?"

"Yes," Lawrence said, and then seemed to notice for the first time that Huston was not in the carriage with them. "Sam, where is Andrew?"

"Now, don't get excited, Talbot," Dean said.

"About what?"

"We recruited a man," Dean said, "and we were sending him to Arizona today."

"When did you recruit him?"

"Yesterday."

"And Andrew is meeting him at the station?"

"Yes."

Lawrence gave Dean a hard look and said, "I gave orders that no one was to be recruited until I got here."

"Orders?" Dean said. "You think you give the orders? We're supposed to be equals, Talbot."

"But we're not, are we, Sam?" Lawrence said. "You and Andrew just are not as smart as I am, are you?"

Dean didn't answer.

"What's he like, the man you recruited?" Lawrence asked. "What's he look like?"

Sam Dean wet his lips and said, "He's big . . . and red-headed."

He watched Talbot Lawrence, waiting for the explosion, and when none came he frowned.

"Very good," Lawrence said finally.

"What?"

"Oh, you and Andrew have blundered mightily, Sam," Lawrence said, "but it's going to work out. When will this man be getting to the station?"

"In about five minutes."

Lawrence leaned forward and shouted to the driver, "Turn this thing around and go back!"

He looked at Dean as the driver turned the vehicle about. "How many men do we have at the station?"

"I have two stationed there," Dean said, "and two men picking up the recruit."

"And then there's the two of us here, and Andrew. You and Andrew are armed, aren't you?"

"Yes, but—"

"I know, Sam," Lawrence said, "we don't usually take an active part, but now that you and Andrew have put our whole operation in danger, we're going to have to save it ourselves."

"It shouldn't be too hard to take care of one man," Dean said, without any trace of confidence in his voice.

"Two men," Lawrence said.

"We only saw one."

"Well, believe me," Lawrence said, "there will be two, and we'll take care of them both."

As his carriage pulled up in front of the station Canyon looked around. He spotted the man he knew as Mr. Jones standing in front of the station door.

"Something wrong?" one of his escorts asked him.

"I'm just looking around, friend," Canyon said. "I've stayed alive this long by knowing what I'm walking into."

"No problem ," the man said. "There's me and Jack here, two men in the station, and one of the bosses."

"I see."

"Let's go," the man said. "You don't want to miss your train."

"No," Canyon said, "I wouldn't want to do that."

He walked to the station door with a man on either side of him.

"Good morning, Mr. O'Grady," the man Canyon knew as Jones said.

"Hey, you can talk?" Canyon marveled.

"I can talk," Jones said, "when I choose to. Shall we go to the train?"

"I get an escort right to the train, huh?"

"We want to make sure you get off safely," Jones said as they walked through the doors. "When you get to Arizona, there will be someone waiting for you."

"With another thousand dollars?"

Jones smiled. "You've gotten two already, Mr. O'Grady. That should hold you for a while."

"Sure," Canyon agreed, "for a while. Tell me, just where in Arizona is it I'm going?"

"You'll know when you get there."

As in Chicago, Canyon became aware that something was happening behind him.

"Stop!" a voice shouted.

"What the hell—" Jones said, turning.

Canyon didn't turn. He simply pushed Jones to one side and shoved one of his two escorts the other way, causing him to stumble. The remaining man said, "Hey, wha—" before Canyon drew his gun and slashed the man across the face with the barrel. The man fell to the floor like a sack of grain.

"Stop him, damn it!"

Canyon recognized the voice as the same one that had called out to them in the Chicago station. It had to be Talbot Lawrence.

Canyon guessed that the man had caught an earlier train. He ran for cover as a volley of shots rang out.

Frank Nolan pulled up in front of the station in a cab and heard the volley of fire from inside. He jumped from the cab with his gun drawn and the driver, seeing this and hearing the gunfire, forgot about getting paid and pulled away as fast as his horse would take him.

Nolan ran through the station door, and hearing the doors open, Sam Dean turned and saw him. All Nolan saw was that Dean had a gun in his hand, and he didn't know that the man was too frightened to fire it.

"Wait, wait, wait, wait . . ." Dean cried out desperately, holding his hands out in front of him, but Nolan didn't wait. He shot the man in the face.

Talbot Lawrence turned quickly and fired. Nolan felt a

searing pain in his hip and fell to the floor. Even from there, however, his eyes searched the station for Canyon O'Grady, whose back he was supposed to be watching.

Talbot Lawrence, who had never shot anyone before, assumed that one bullet was all it took to kill someone, and he turned away from Nolan to run across the station toward Canyon.

Nolan, alive because of Lawrence's inexperience, pushed himself to a sitting position and located Canyon, who was pinned down behind some luggage. Two men were firing at him, and now Lawrence was on his way to join in.

Nolan tried to ignore the pain in his hip. He raised his gun and fired. . . .

Canyon saw Nolan burst into the station, shoot the man he knew as Smith, and then get shot by Lawrence, but it was all peripheral, because he was returning fire at the same time.

The man he'd struck was still down on the floor, but the others were firing at him. Canyon couldn't see Jones and didn't know he had taken cover behind a counter and was taking no part in the gunplay.

On the other hand, Talbot Lawrence was running across the floor after having shot Nolan, and was also firing at Canyon.

Canyon could have shot Lawrence dead in his tracks, but he wanted to keep the man alive. He needed to find out where in Arizona the Assassination Club was training its personnel.

At that moment he saw Nolan prop himself up and raise his gun, and he knew with absolute certainty that Nolan was going to shoot Lawrence in the back.

"Frank, no!" he shouted, but Nolan had just pulled the trigger.

As the bullet struck Talbot Lawrence in the back a look of shock and surprise came over the man's face. His legs went out from under him, and his momentum threw him to the floor, where he proceeded to skid several feet before coming to a stop in a heap.

"Shit!" Canyon swore.

The three men who had been firing at Canyon now saw an easier target. Nolan was still sitting on the floor in front of the station entrance, and had no cover whatsoever. That, coupled with the fact that he had just shot their boss, caused them to shift their attention from Canyon to Frank Nolan.

Canyon, seeing this, knew that Nolan was a dead man if he couldn't give him cover. As the three gunmen turned to fire at Nolan, and Nolan began to fire back, Canyon stood and fired at them as well. He cut one man down with his first shot, and another man was felled by a bullet from Nolan's gun. The third man, confused as to which enemy to shoot at first, was struck by two bullets—one from each man's gun—and fell to the floor.

The quiet that filled the station at that moment was deafening. Station personnel and passengers, who had taken cover when the shooting started, remained where they were, not yet daring to move.

Canyon moved out from behind the luggage and hurried over to where Lawrence lay facedown. He leaned over the man and checked for a pulse. Finding none, he walked over to where Nolan was.

"How bad, Frank?" he asked.

"Bad enough to hurt," Nolan said between clenched teeth, "but not bad enough to kill me . . . I don't think."

"Well, don't die until I have a chance to kill you."

"What?" Nolan asked, puzzled. "I just saved your bacon, O'Grady."

"You killed Lawrence," Canyon said. "We needed to find out where in Arizona they're training their men. If we don't know that, we can't shut them down permanently. How are we going to find out now?"

"Will he do?" Nolan asked, pointing behind Canyon.

Canyon turned and saw the man he knew as Jones, who

he would later find out was Andrew Huston. He'd forgotten about him.

The man had come out from behind the counter. He was standing up now, his hands raised, his gun on the floor in front of him, unfired. Both he and Sam Dean had been too frightened to participate in the firefight. Now that it was over, he was looking to surrender.

"Don't s-shoot," he stammered across the station. "I'll tell you anything you want to know."

Canyon looked down at Nolan, who had a self-satisfied expression on his face, and said, "You're a lucky bastard, Frank Nolan."

"Whataya mean lucky?" Nolan asked. "I had a plan all along."

RIDING THE WESTERN TRAIL

☐ THE TRAILSMAN #99: CAMP SAINT LUCIFER by Jon Sharpe.
(164431—$3.50)

☐ THE TRAILSMAN #100: RIVERBOAT GOLD by Jon Sharpe.
(164814—$3.95)

☐ THE TRAILSMAN #101: SHOSHONI SPIRITS by Jon Sharpe.
(165489—$3.50)

☐ THE TRAILSMAN #103: SECRET SIXGUNS by Jon Sharpe.
(166116—$3.50)

☐ THE TRAILSMAN #104: COMANCHE CROSSING by Jon Sharpe.
(167058—$3.50)

☐ THE TRAILSMAN #105: BLACK HILLS BLOOD by Jon Sharpe.
(167260—$3.50)

☐ THE TRAILSMAN #106: SIERRA SHOOT-OUT by Jon Sharpe.
(167465—$3.50)

☐ THE TRAILSMAN #107: GUNSMOKE GULCH by Jon Sharpe.
(168038—$3.50)

☐ THE TRAILSMAN #108: PAWNEE BARGAIN by Jon Sharpe.
(168577—$3.50)

☐ THE TRAILSMAN #109: LONE STAR LIGHTNING by Jon Sharpe.
(168801—$3.50)

Buy them at your local bookstore or use this convenient coupon for ordering.

NEW AMERICAN LIBRARY
P.O. Box 999, Bergenfield, New Jersey 07621

Please send me the books I have checked above.
I am enclosing $_____ (please add $2.00 to cover postage and handling).
Send check or money order (no cash or C.O.D.'s) or charge by Mastercard or
VISA (with a $15.00 minimum). Prices and numbers are subject to change without
notice.

Card #_____ Exp. Date _____
Signature_____
Name_____
Address_____
City _____ State _____ Zip Code _____
For faster service when ordering by credit card call **1-800-253-6476**
Allow a minimum of 4-6 weeks for delivery. This offer is subject to change without notice.